I0716325

MURDER ON THE GUADALUPE

A Fen Maguire Mystery

MURDER ON THE GUADALUPE

A Fen Maguire Mystery

BRUCE HAMMACK

Chapter One

F our loud knocks sounded on the door to the upscale condo overlooking the Guadalupe River. The coffee cup with the day's first sip of hot eye-opener was on its way to Fen's lips when the unexpected racket caused him to flinch. In the time it took to blink, he'd scalded his chin, spilled coffee on the glass-topped table, and splattered the T-shirt he'd slept in. A fair amount of coffee had also traveled down to his sleep shorts, causing him to spring up and bellow a made-up word expressing extreme displeasure.

He jerked the leading edge of the paper towels hanging from under a kitchen cabinet and the entire roll came down. It hit the counter, tumbled off the edge, and continued unrolling, leaving a wake of white on the kitchen floor.

By the time he arrived at the front door, four more knocks had sounded, even more insistent than their predecessors. Mumbles of displeasure flowed as Fen twisted the doorknob and tried to jerk open the barrier. It held fast. Not only had he failed to release the dead bolt, but a brass safety chain also stared back at him as if to mock and add an extra insult to his bleary-eyed attempt to complete simple tasks.

Fen's thoughts ran through a short list of who might be disturbing his early-morning ritual and why. The first suspect who crossed his mind was Bailey. "What kind of trouble has she gotten herself into?" he asked, though no one was there to answer. At eighteen years, and unrepentant about much of her checkered past, she seemed the most likely candidate.

The only other possibility that came to his caffeine-deprived mind was someone playing an early-morning prank. This didn't seem likely given the quality of the condo complex and the average age of the residents being five years past retirement.

It didn't matter to him who was at the door. They'd get an earful about giving a man adequate time to answer. The metallic sounds of unlocking, unfastening, and turning a handle preceded the door flying open. Before him stood a young man wearing an oversized uniform of a City of Kerrville police patrolman with all the accoutrements. Everything hung on him as if he was a metal coat hanger.

"What do you want?" snapped Fen.

The man's Adam's apple traveled up and back down. "Sheriff Maguire?"

"Not anymore." He let out a sigh that mixed curiosity with a hint of regret for snapping at such a pitifully skinny young man. "Out of curiosity, who wants to know and why?"

"Uh... Chief Strange sent me to get you."

"I don't know anyone by that name." Fen tried to close the door, but the young man was quicker than expected and had his boot between the door and the frame.

Undeterred, the officer elaborated on the identity of the person responsible for spoiling a perfectly good June morning.

"Ben Strange is the new chief of police. The city hired him two weeks ago."

"This isn't a social call, is it?"

The deputy shook his head and pointed to the river. "A body washed up on the bank of the Guadalupe about a quarter of a mile past the bridge on Sidney Baker Street."

"Isn't that Highway 16?"

The officer nodded again. "It's the main road that goes north to Fredericksburg." He took a breath. "Chief Strange told me if I came back without you, I'd be using a mop with a six-inch handle to clean the holding cells."

The ringing of Fen's cell phone saved him from telling the cop that short-handled mopping sounded like a personal problem. If he'd had his morning cup of coffee and talked to a photo of his late wife, he might be in the mood to talk. It was a morning ritual he kept, and even the report of a potential homicide didn't rise to the level of giving him the desire to break his routine.

With a step back, he waved the officer in and took long strides down a short hall toward the bedroom to answer the call in private.

The ringing stopped when he punched the green button. "Chuck, what are you up to? Lawyers don't make phone calls this early."

"They do when a well-connected person disappears and the police find a body fitting her description a few days later."

Fen groaned. "That explains the cop in the living room with instructions to take me to Chief Strange... dead or alive."

This brought a laugh from Chuck, followed by, "You impressed some important people with how you and your team solved the last two murders. Ben Strange is young, but those same people want to see him succeed."

Fen thought back to the two murders Chuck alluded to.

The first involved a small-time drug dealer in Newman County. Fen noticed his body floating down the Brazos River and soon found himself embroiled in a murder case that an incompetent sheriff couldn't handle. The second investigation started as an extortion scheme against local truckers in East Texas. Things changed when a man was murdered while playing paintball.

Fen turned his attention back to his friend and chuckled. "My team? That's a stretch. I have a hard-headed newspaper reporter and a young artist whose mouth engages before her brain."

"You'll need both of them again. Lou is packing as we speak. As usual, she'll do research, keeping you informed of what she discovers, and filing stories with the press."

Levity was missing from Chuck's voice now. It was time to pay attention. "What about Bailey?" asked Fen.

"There's a good chance Bailey will be a big help to you. We don't have a positive ID yet, but a woman named Jewell Key went missing three nights ago."

"There's a student in the art class I'm teaching at the local university named Candice Key. In fact, I met Candice and her mother on Friday when the students checked in. Both are hard to forget. Jewell impressed me as being an expensive woman who's used to having her way. She let me know right off how many contests Candice has won and that one of her works is on display at the Amon Carter Museum of Western Art in Fort Worth."

"Yeah, that sounds like Jewell. What she said may or may not be one-hundred percent true. The story on Jewell is that she's married and divorced enough rich men to buy what she wants."

"How many?" asked Fen as he pulled off his stained undershirt and pitched it on the floor of the closet.

"Five. Two are successful entrepreneurs and another owns four sections of land with oil and cattle between Kerrville and Mexico. Next, there's a politician whose name you'd recognize. Finally, there's one who inherited ten acres of land."

"Ten acres isn't much to brag about."

"It is when some of Houston's tallest buildings are on them."

Fen whispered the real estate mantra, "Location, location, location." He paused long enough to take a breath. "Who can we expect trouble from?"

Chuck didn't immediately answer, then Fen heard him swallow. Unlike himself, Chuck was probably enjoying a nice cup of hot coffee at his desk. After an audible "Ah," he said, "A better question might be, which one won't demand quick results."

The officer hollered from the other side of the closed bedroom door. "Are you 'bout ready? Chief Strange wanted me to get you down to the river as quick as possible."

Chuck spoke next. "It sounds like you need to go. Good luck and be careful with this case. If it's Jewell, she's rubbed shoulders with most of the upper crust of the state." He took a breath. "Come to think of it, she's rubbed more than shoulders."

Fen pushed the red icon as Chuck roared with laughter at his own joke.

Three minutes later, he opened the passenger's door to the waiting patrol car. It had been months since he'd worked a homicide and he needed to shift gears mentally. The scream of the siren on the way to the crime scene helped him refocus.

Chapter Two

It didn't take long to arrive in a parking lot overlooking the river, near the city center of Kerrville, Texas. A platoon of vehicles from multiple agencies and city departments, many with staccato lights activated, announced the summer day had started on a tragic note. The thin officer, Brent Craven, led the way past a gauntlet of uniforms, down two long flights of concrete steps, and past first responders standing around with hands in pockets.

Fen stopped at the bottom of the steps and took in the scene. To his right stood a short concrete dam that slowed the flow of the river enough to form a wide lake upstream. Water spilled over it at a good clip into a canyon with a steep bank on one side and a gentle slope on the other. He noticed a walking path traversing the far bank with what looked like a discarded section of a blue tarp under a stubby oak tree.

To the left, at the base of the near bank, officers had strung yellow police tape from the branch of a scrawny bush clinging to the riverbank to a more substantial tree in a dry portion of the river bed. Two grim-faced city officers guarded the barrier as if someone might steal it. They reminded him of bouncers standing at the door of a nightclub. The two raised the tape at the same time to allow Fen to enter alone.

He continued along a flat stone ledge until he came to a semi-circle of three men. The uniform with silver-colored stars on the collar, a badge, and pistol on the hip gave away the identity of the chief of police. He wasn't a tall man, but stood erect, giving him the appearance of authority. Brown eyes locked on Fen. Chief Strange closed the distance, lifted his right hand, and offered a handshake.

"Ben Strange," said the newly-minted leader of Kerrville's police department. "I hope you don't mind taking a look and giving me your thoughts." He cut his eyes to the two men looking at a body. She lay face down in a pool of calm water. Chief Strange lowered his voice to a whisper. "The fire chief will have his team remove the body after the justice of the peace determines the need for an autopsy."

Fen lowered his voice to match Ben's. "Who's the man dabbing his head with a handkerchief?"

"Mayor Fred Bean. He's a little high-strung."

"Is he your boss?"

"No... and yes. The city council hires and fires, but he has plenty of influence with them."

Fen compared his work history of ten years as a highway patrolman and another ten as sheriff of Newman County, a central Texas county rich in agriculture and oil, with the Brazos River running through it. In Texas sheriffs are elected, so he never had to answer to a committee, a fact that he was grateful for.

He turned to face the dam, away from the two men, so the sound of the river would drown out his voice as he asked Chief Strange, "What have you done so far?"

"Secured the crime scene and sent officers to each side of the bank from here to the dam looking for evidence."

Fen gave a nod. "That's good. Make sure they check out that guy on the opposite bank sleeping under the tarp."

"Are you sure there's someone under it?"

"Look at the shape. It's someone sleeping or a huge blue sausage. The storm last night didn't last but it came down hard. It's possible the victim went over the dam and someone upstream noticed something."

"I'll expand the search area. Anything else?"

"I'd look farther downstream, too. Do you have a positive ID on the victim?"

"Not yet, but if it's Jewell Key, I'll need to schedule a press conference."

He gave Ben a hard look. "I'm here to give you a hand from behind the scenes. The emphasis is on me staying out of sight and out of the press. I can find out more by being an artist and teacher than I can by flashing a private investigator's badge."

Their conversation came to an abrupt end as the mayor and fire chief approached. After handshakes and introductions, Mayor Bean took the lead. "I'm sorry we're meeting under such circumstances, but it's a pleasure to meet you, Mr. Maguire. Your reputation as an artist goes without saying, and we're all delighted that you're here to help the university with its summer program for gifted high school students. It's good to see you still have a hand in law enforcement."

Fen hooked his thumbs in the front pockets of his jeans. "After twenty years of wearing a badge, I hope I learned a thing or two. Chief Strange asked me to take a quick peek at things. You know, out of an abundance of caution. I'm happy to report he has all the bases covered, just in case this turns out to be something more than an accidental drowning. I understand the Guadalupe has quite the reputation for flash floods."

The mayor was quick to respond. "It's not nearly as bad in town now as it was in the old days. The two low-water dams made a world of difference, but things can still get dicey past the second dam." He pointed to water spilling over the barrier.

The fire chief, a grizzled man in his late fifties, took his turn. "Swift-flowing water can make identifying a body difficult. We try to leave bodies wherever the river takes them until we get the go-ahead. Of course, that's not always possible with rising water."

Fen asked, "Has anyone moved the body?"

"EMTs checked for a pulse, but that's all."

A shout sounded from upstream, close to the dam. Heads turned to see a police officer waving her arms. The chief's radio came alive with word that she'd found a purse.

The chief keyed his microphone. "Unless it's going to float away, don't touch it. Take preliminary photos with your phone and walk out in the same footprints you made going in."

Fen didn't say it, but the purse likely held the victim's identity. The chances of a body and a purse in the same general vicinity without the purse belonging to the dead woman were almost zero.

It wasn't long before a man and woman dressed in white coveralls eased into the area the officer had vacated. They snapped photos of the rocky ground as they went, placed a yellow plastic marker beside the purse, and took photographs from various angles.

The chief's radio crackled to life again. "Do you want us to bring you the purse?"

"Bring it, and get photos of the body before the JP gets here."

It wasn't long before the two-person team approached. The quartet of Fen, Chief Strange, the fire chief, and the mayor looked on as the female forensics officer opened the waterlogged clutch purse. She extracted a driver's license and announced, "Rose Cunningham. The address is San Antonio."

The mayor let out what sounded like a huge breath of relief, followed by a whisper. "At least it isn't Jewell."

Fen spoke without thinking. "It's still a suspicious death."

Chief Strange nodded in agreement and added, "Jewell is still missing, and now we have the potential of two crimes."

The chief and Fen took out their phones and snapped photos of the driver's license. The woman replaced the license into the wallet and slipped the purse into a plastic evidence bag held by her partner. She went to the edge of the rock ledge and began snapping photos of the body.

A sense of partial relief seemed to settle over the grim scene. The woman at the river's edge wasn't the missing woman of notoriety. Good news for the mayor and chief of police... at least for the moment.

The chief's radio came to life again with an officer giving his call sign and that of the chief. Ben cast his gaze to the opposite bank. The blue tarp was now in a crumpled pile beside someone sitting upright with his back against the trunk of a stubby oak. "What do you have?" asked the chief.

"It's Ray-Ray. I can't get anything out of him."

"Take him in for questioning."

"He probably won't be able to say anything until this afternoon. There're two empty wine bottles beside him."

"Book him for public intoxication. Maybe we'll get lucky and when he sobers up, he might recall seeing something last night."

Fen pulled the chief aside and whispered, "I didn't see any cash in the wallet. Since you have your forensic crew here, you might have them check for evidence of an assault or robbery."

"Good idea," said the chief. "I'll have all Ray-Ray's clothes bagged and tagged when he gets to jail."

"Is Ray-Ray a regular customer of yours?"

The chief nodded. "Mr. Raymond Ray, local drunk and drug addict. He's also a street musician who can play and sing anything you want to hear. He's one of those guys who plays and sounds stone-cold-sober until he puts his guitar in its case. Then the grape juice hits him and he acts a fool."

"Any violence?"

"Only when he's high and someone hassles him."

The chief's radio sounded again with a second message from the officer with Ray-Ray. "Chief, I found credit cards and over a hundred dollars on Ray-Ray."

"Do you have an evidence bag?"

"Uh... no."

"You'd better be wearing gloves."

"Uh..."

"Stay there and don't compromise the evidence any more than you already have. Sergeant Ramirez is on his way."

Fen and the police chief shifted their gaze to the concrete steps leading from the parking lot to the river bank. Chief Strange said, "There's Judge Brown."

"The JP?"

"He's a cautious man of few words."

The justice of the peace bypassed Fen and the chief after acknowledging their presence with a nod. He clambered down the ledge overlooking the body and broke his silence by asking, "Are you finished taking photos of the body *in situ?*"

The woman wearing white coveralls gave a positive answer.

After pulling up the dead woman's blouse and examining her back and neck, he tugged the blouse down and turned the body over. Fen stood where he had a good look at her face. She was an attractive woman with long black hair that the JP eased away from her face and throat. Fen thought it remarkable that the woman in the river looked so much like Candice's mother.

The JP stood aside as the woman with the camera snapped additional photos. "Get close-ups of her throat."

The camera clicked several times.

Judge Brown turned to the men on the ledge above him. "She'll need to go to San Antonio for an autopsy. I'm ruling this a suspicious death."

That did not surprise Fen. The purple bruising on her neck suggested strangulation.

With his job done, the JP received a hand up from the fire chief. Once on the ledge, the judge asked, "Any idea who this woman is?"

Chief Strange gave him the tentative identification and said he'd text him the photo he took of her driver's license. Judge Brown thanked him, then had a quick word with the mayor and the two left together, discussing who would pay for breakfast.

The fire chief took over recovering the body. Fen and Chief Strange moved away as a crew of firefighters came with a basket gurney and began the grim task of loading and carrying out the woman believed to be Rose Cunningham.

Fen kept his voice low. "Did you take a good look at the victim?"

The chief nodded. "A very attractive woman. Such a shame."

"That's not all," said Fen. "Part of being an artist is studying physical details, especially faces. I met Jewell Friday at the university, then took my time looking at her photo in the local paper when she went missing." He pointed to the woman being covered. "She could be Jewell's twin sister."

The chief's head snapped to look at the body. "Are you sure?"

"There were cuts on her face from bouncing across the rocks, but take those away and she's a dead ringer for Mrs. Key."

Puffed-out cheeks showed the chief understood the gravity of Fen's words. "What are the chances of a missing big-wig having a doppelgänger?"

"Not good, but it's possible."

"Do you think Jewell's still alive?"

Fen lifted his shoulders and let them drop. "Every day that passes lowers the chances."

Chapter Three

The steam in Fen's shower was thick as a London fog. He never enjoyed dealing with death and used the extra-hot water to sweat out the images that seemed to have seeped into his skin. His discomfort with death increased exponentially after Sally died. It always puzzled him that he'd chosen a career as a state trooper, in which responding to grisly traffic accidents was as common as allergies in the spring. Being a sheriff was more of an administrative job, until it came to homicides and serious assaults. The voters in his rural Central Texas county looked to him to be the man in charge of those investigations, even though a detective should have been. He'd pass off as much of the investigations as he could, but the buck stopped at his badge, which meant he had to know every detail of the crimes and take an active role in solving them.

Here he was without a badge other than that of a private investigator, still being called upon by his attorney and some influential people who want to keep justice flowing in Texas. He knew he could say no and paint landscapes to his heart's content, but something inside him loved the hunt and capture of the most dangerous beast on the planet: his fellow man... or woman.

Once the opened pores had discharged enough sweat and sin, he turned the handle on the shower to cold water. He hated and, at the same time, loved the sensation that pricks of bone-chilling water brought. Was it a form of self-flagellation? Perhaps, but the temporary discomfort made him feel alive. It was much better than the sleep-walking through life he'd practiced after Sally died.

Clean and somehow purified, he dried with a fluffy, over-sized, white towel. He shaved and combed his thick, brown hair, ignoring the strands of gray illegally parked over his ears. Today would be a day spent with high school students, their sketch pads and artists' pencils in hand. Paintbrushes would come after they had a scene anchored firmly in their minds.

The absence of acrylics and oils in today's agenda meant it was relatively safe to wear his new jeans and the Hawaiian shirt his housekeeper, Thelma, had given him for Christmas. It was a bright, gaudy, fashion statement of summer, and he loved it, especially when he was knocking around his four-thousand-acre ranch. His cattle didn't recognize him the first time he wore it but soon grew used to sailboats, palm trees, and hula dancers.

He reheated a cup of abandoned coffee in the microwave and restarted his day by telling Sally, his late wife, what had happened at the river and what his plans were for the day. "Good morning, honey. Sorry I didn't speak to you sooner, but you already know what happened." He paused and looked up. "At least someone up there knows. I'm still not clear on how that omniscience stuff works for people after we pass on. Do you know everything, or is it just the Big Guy?"

He took a sip of coffee. This time, he didn't burn his chin or scald any other parts. He chuckled. "I suppose you and your buddies up there got a good laugh from watching me this morning."

The only noise was the sound of birds and traffic.

"It's the first day of instruction and I'm taking the students down to the river to do sketches. I think this morning we'll go across the road running in front of Schreiner University. That's Highway 27. This afternoon I'll take them farther upstream to Louise Hays Park and Tranquility Island. They can have their choice of painting a serene lake or the rugged landscape of the river below the lake. I think it will be interesting to see which one the students choose. I'm betting Bailey will choose the rough country and fast-moving water. That seems to fit her personality better."

Another swig of coffee went down and brought a sense of warm normalcy to him. "I'll need to call Chuck and Candy in a few minutes, and also talk to Lou Cooper. She won't like it when she learns it wasn't Jewell in the river this morning, but only because the victim isn't a celebrity. There's still a murder to solve and, unless Jewell surfaced in the last forty-five minutes, she's still missing." He tilted his head and slanted his eyes toward the ceiling. "You don't know where she is, do you?"

Silence.

"I thought that's what you'd say." His coffee was getting cold. "I told Bailey to get to know Jewell's daughter, Candice. She wasn't excited about the assignment. I don't think Bailey has much in common with any of the girls here, other than they're all talented artists. Who knows, she may make a lifelong friend during the next two weeks."

Fen closed out the session by kissing the tip of his index finger, placing it over the lips of his former wife's photo, and moving the picture back to the nightstand by his bed.

His phone rang before he could call Chuck. Instead of his

attorney's name showing up, it was a call from Candy, Chuck's wife. "I hope I didn't interfere with your time with Sally."

"I just put her picture back on the nightstand."

"Good. I told Chuck the next time he called you before 7:00 a.m. he'd be on the couch for a week. And now it turns out the victim wasn't Jewell after all."

Fen moved toward the kitchen and another cup of coffee. "Has she surfaced?"

"Not yet. The last anyone saw or heard from her, she was staying at the Y.O. Ranch Hotel and Conference Center in Kerrville. She's booked until the classes you're teaching end in two weeks."

"Oh," said Fen, not trying to hide his mixed feelings.

Candy must have heard the hesitation in his voice. "You don't sound thrilled that it wasn't Jewell in the river."

"It's not that. If she shows up hale and hearty, I have a feeling she'll come in like a big military helicopter and hover over her daughter, and me."

"The report I have from Lou says that's her pattern."

"Lou's already doing background reports?"

"She worked on them all day yesterday, but still has a lot of ground to cover."

Fen poured another cup of coffee. He placed it in the microwave and pressed the button for an express cooking time of one minute. "I was going to call Lou and give her the latest."

"Tell me first."

"Don't you already know that it wasn't Jewell in the river?"

"So far, that's all we know."

"I'll text you the photo I took of the probable homicide victim."

"Probable?"

"She could have fallen into the river and drowned, then gone over the spillway. I think it's unlikely because of the bruising on her neck." The microwave announced the coffee was hot. "Either way, she looks a lot like Jewell. The J.P. ordered an autopsy and she should be on I-10 going to San Antonio about now."

"Be sure to send the photos to Lou also. She'll start background research on the victim after she gets checked into her hotel."

"Where's she staying?"

"At the Y.O. If Jewell shows up, she'll be able to monitor her part-time."

Fen took the steaming coffee from the microwave. Not wanting a repeat of the morning, he placed it on the counter without spilling a drop.

"Before you go," said Candy. "How's Bailey?"

"She wasn't happy about having to share a room with another student but brightened when I told her to keep her eyes and ears open for anything concerning Jewell's disappearance. She'll be itching to get involved in a homicide if I'm asked to pursue this death."

"That's between you, Lou, Bailey, and the local authorities. The person of interest to Chuck and me is Jewell. She knows a lot of things about important people. Things that could cause a lot of damage."

Fen spoke as he carefully moved his coffee to the living room, making sure he didn't slosh the contents. "The locals already have a suspect in custody. Who knows, they may have the case solved by sundown."

Even as Fen said the words, they sounded like the tinkle of cheap foreign coins. Something about the two women looking so much alike told him this case fit into a different category. Finding a dead look-alike to a missing person didn't bode well for a quick solution. No. The cases of the woman in the Guadalupe and the missing woman of wealth and influence made him pause before he spoke in a serious, guarded tone.

"Candy, there's something you and Chuck should know about the woman in the river. She's a dead ringer for Jewell. The chief of police used the word 'doppelgänger.' You know I study faces and I would have sworn the woman in the water was Jewell if the cops hadn't found a purse with the woman's driver's license in it."

A three-second pause followed. Candy cleared her throat. "That puts a different light on the situation, doesn't it."

It wasn't a question, but a statement of fact.

Fen watched the steam rise from his mug. "The more I think about it, the less I like what I'm thinking."

"I'll let Chuck know." Another momentary pause. "How will you proceed?"

"There's not much we can do until Jewell surfaces." He let out a soft groan. "That was a poor choice of words, considering where the woman was this morning. I'll have Lou do a thorough analysis of today's victim and see if there's any link between her and Jewell. Bailey will try to befriend Jewell's daughter, Candice. I'll also try to press Candice for information, but she impressed me as a tough nut to crack."

"Just like her mother," said Candy as she took in a deep breath. "Keep us posted if anything changes."

"Will do," said Fen. "Tell Chuck to keep his boots off the desk."

"Ha! I'd have to break both his legs for that to happen."

Fen traded the now-silent phone for his cup of coffee sitting on a glass-topped coffee table with metal legs. He took a sip and again swapped out coffee for his cell phone and told it to call Lou.

She answered with highway noise in the background.

"Let me catch you up on what's going on," said Fen. For the

next fifteen minutes, he relayed all he'd seen and his suspicions. The call ended with Lou saying, "If this is a case of mistaken identity, it won't make much of a story. Are you letting that overactive creative streak get away from you?"

"You could be right," said Fen.

"Is there any chance it could be Jewell with a fake ID? After all you said the home address on it is San Antonio. That's where she lives."

"I thought of that, too. The chief of police may be new to the job, but he's enough on the ball to be cautious until they have a positive ID."

"Hmm," said Lou, which could mean many things. "What's that retired cop's gut telling you?"

"To wait and not make a fool of myself. What's your sixth sense as a crime reporter saying to you?"

"To write three stories and have them ready to publish. The first will tell of a woman from San Antonio whom they found dead in the Guadalupe River under suspicious circumstances. The second will be a follow-up on Jewell's mysterious disappearance."

A horn blared, and Lou screamed.

"What happened?" asked Fen as he gripped the phone and listened intently.

"Stupid white-tailed deer!" shouted Lou. "You'll live a lot longer if you stay off the road."

The crisis soon passed and Fen smiled. "Close call?"

"She must be half cat the way she jumped. I know I scared her out of one of her nine lives."

"Where were we when you were so rudely interrupted?"

Lou remained silent for a few seconds before she said, "I was on the verge of telling you my idea for writing a third story and having it ready to go. It would be about a woman who looked enough like Jewell to pass as her. An unknown assailant mistook the woman for Jewell, killed her, and left her body in the Guadalupe."

"That sounds like a story that will sell."

"It sounds like a fairy tale to me, but I'll write it just in case."

Chapter Four

Despite the morning's flurry of activity, Fen arrived at the classroom in the art department only twelve minutes late for his 9:00 a.m. class with the gifted high school students. A woman he'd met on the preceding Friday stood guarding the door with arms crossed and gray hair pulled back in a tight bun.

"Good morning, Mrs. Dillworth," he said while showing her a broad smile.

She didn't move. A scowl remained on her face and she didn't return the greeting. "If you plan on being habitually late for classes, I'll need to alter my schedule."

Taken aback he asked, "What schedule is that? I thought the students were my responsibility from 9:00 a.m. until evening."

She tapped a wristwatch. "Punctuality, Mr. Maguire, is a hallmark of moral character."

Fen thought she must be kidding so he quipped, "I heard it's a sign of obsessive-compulsive behavior."

"Hardly." Her nostrils flared. "What are you going to do about the students' behavior this weekend?"

He shrugged. "What did they do?"

She huffed out a burst of air. "I sent you an email."

"I rarely check email on weekends. It interrupts my painting. I prefer phone calls or texts. Much quicker."

"That's not acceptable."

He shrugged in a way that communicated she might have to accept his answer even if she considered it unacceptable. He then said, "Why don't you tell me what the students did?"

"Very well. There's evidence that some of the boys smoked cigarettes and I have my suspicions that a girl has whatever they call those things that they suck on and blow a cloud of white out of their lungs."

He scratched his chin. "Do you mean she was vaping?"

She nodded. "That's not all. The bathing suits the girls brought are totally unacceptable and one student dresses like a vampire."

Fen had heard enough. "Mrs. Dillworth, my contract calls for me to teach, not babysit. Some of my students have already graduated from high school. There's not one who hasn't earned dual credit. These are some of the most gifted and creative students in the state. It doesn't surprise me one bit that they're stretching the boundaries, trying to find themselves."

Her face reminded him of a granite bust, cold and hard. "I should have expected this from an artist. No sense of propriety. Very well. The students are yours to supervise as you see fit when they're outside the dorm. You're not to interfere with me or my methods once they enter my area of responsibility."

She stepped aside and walked away with the stiffness of a drill sergeant.

Shrugging off the unpleasant encounter, Fen entered a room full of chattering students. He expected Bailey to be sitting on the back row, and she didn't disappoint him. Learning about the normal things taught in school, or anything else, had seldom taken place within the walls of a classroom for her. This didn't mean she lacked reading or math skills. High intuition and a mastery of basics gave her a leg up on most people. Also, she'd completed one semester of college while helping him solve a murder in East Texas earlier this year.

The other students, however, chose the seats close to the front. They seemed eager to either learn from or impress the teacher whose paintings were turning heads and commanding impressive returns. He hoped they were there to learn. One lesson he intended to teach them was it took a long time to build a reputation. Most shouldn't expect it to be more than a part-time income for years. The expression *starving artist* held more truth than most people realized.

"Good morning," he began as bright eyes looked on expectantly. "My name is Fen Maguire, and I'll be guiding you for the next two weeks on your journey to become better artists. We need to get some things straight between us before we begin this journey. In case you didn't notice, this is the campus of a private university, not a high school. I'm going to treat you as if you were a college student. If you sleep late and miss classes, it's your loss. I don't take roll. If you don't want my advice, so be it. Sleep in and enjoy an expensive vacation."

He paused. "Like I said, I'm treating you like an adult. That means you're on your own getting along with everyone."

A scratchy boy's voice came from the crowd. "Are you talking about Mrs. Dillworth?"

"I'm talking about all students, staff, people in town—everyone." He grinned at the young man. "You must be the one she busted with cigarettes."

Another young man confirmed Fen's suspicions by punching the cigarette smoker in the arm and saying, "You were here two days and Mrs. Dillworth busted you."

Fen raised his voice and continued, "After today, you'll

have only one assignment: Produce the best landscape painting you're capable of. A team of judges will determine the top three entries."

A hand went up. "Will you be a judge?"

Fen gave his head a firm shake. "I'm happy to say that I won't be, at least not directly. The judges may, or may not, ask me questions about each of you."

"Like what?" asked a strikingly attractive brunette in the first row. It was Candice, the daughter of the missing woman.

"Like if anyone tried to bribe me or influence me in any way."

Bailey let out a giggle from the back of the room while the girl with the designer bag at her feet pursed pouting lips.

Fen issued a toothy smile. "You'll find everything you need for today's assignment on the table at the front of the room. This morning we're going to cross the highway and spread out along the bank of the Guadalupe. Walk as far as you want in either direction but use your time wisely. The only things you'll need to bring today are a sketch pad, pencils, and your cell phone. You'll be sketching the river from at least three different angles. Be sure you take plenty of photos. At noon we'll come back for lunch."

Some students typed notes into their phones as Fen continued, "At one o'clock, a van will take us to Louise Hays Park. For any who don't know, it's near the center of town. You choose which side of the lake you want to sketch. You'll have another three hours to make three more sketches, each from a different viewpoint. By nine o'clock tomorrow morning, you must decide which sketch you want to turn into a completed work of art."

A hand went up from a boy in the second row who was trying to grow hair on his chin and not succeeding very well. "Do you have any tips for choosing the best place or angle?"

"I do, but I'd like to hear from the class how some of you would do it."

Bailey's hand went up, but Fen ignored her. She'd been under his tutelage for the past nine months and even lived in an apartment over his garage that had its own small art studio. Enough time to know the answers to his questions. This unusual relationship came about when the body of her murdered uncle washed up on Fen's property along the Brazos River. She helped him solve that murder and another a few months ago. Also, she and Fen had a successful spring selling their works of art at fairs and festivals, mainly in East Texas.

A hand eased upward from a plain-faced girl in the third row. "I always consider how light will influence my paintings. I'm a huge fan of Thomas Kinkade."

"Good answer. Anyone else care to say what they'll consider?"

Two more hands shot up. "Commercially speaking, spring scenes are the most popular. I'll probably introduce spring wildflowers, even if none are in bloom."

A girl wearing all black said, "Enough with the sunshine and unicorns. Life is hard and so is nature. Mine will show a storm rolling in or something dead."

Candice, the attractive girl in the front row, spoke without raising her hand. "I didn't come here to waste time when we could sketch and paint. Now that we've heard from the novices, what is your advice, Mr. Maguire?"

He sat on the edge of the desk and scanned the room. "Each of you gave excellent answers. I can tell that some of you have already developed a particular style or motif, but think about this: you'll have six sketches to choose from." He pointed at each student who'd responded as he said, "You can make some joyful with flowers, or play with the effects of light, even to the point of excess, or make something dark and brooding.

The question you'll need to answer is which one of the six sketches will you choose and why? Find the why behind your choice and you'll produce something good."

He had their attention so he teased them with a dramatic pause. "Try this and see if it works. Lay all six sketches in front of you tonight. Look at them for as long as it takes before one of them stands out to you. Painting is an alchemy of skill and passion. If you don't rush through selecting the best scene for you, one of the six will stand out. Sometimes I can almost hear my sketches calling out to me. Think perspective and story. Great paintings tell a story."

Candice rolled her eyes. "I didn't think an ex-cop would be a mystic."

He smiled. "People can surprise you." He stood and said, "The sketch pads and pencils are on the table. Be careful crossing the highway. I'd hate to lose any of you on the first day."

As the students walked by to pick up their supplies, he followed Candice out the door. "Can you wait a minute, Candice?"

She stopped and turned around. Perfectly plucked eyebrows raised. He guided her down the hallway far enough so the other students couldn't hear. "I saw a report this morning that your mother is missing. Are you all right to do today's assignment?"

She answered with a snort and a coquettish smile. "Mom's not missing. She doesn't want to be found. All part of the game."

"What game is that?"

She grinned. "You're the ex-cop turned private detective. Figure it out."

Fen smiled but didn't respond otherwise. Candice turned and joined the other students filing out of the classroom. Bailey was the last to leave. She walked slowly, well behind the other students. He spoke in a hushed tone as she joined him. "Make sure you get to know Candice. We may have a murder to solve."

"It may be more than one if Candice doesn't stay away from me."

"The police found a woman who looks a lot like Candice's mom in the river this morning. Don't make an enemy out of Candice until we know more."

"I hope you realize you're asking me to play nice with a rattlesnake."

"More than that. Make friends with her."

"How do I do that when I can't stand her?"

"It's called acting. Think of it as a painting in motion."

"I'm not that good of an artist or an actor. She's sneaky-smart. She'll see right through me."

Fen wondered how to play this unexpected hand. If Candice knew him, that meant she, and likely her mother, had done an internet search on him. It was also likely that Candice already knew Bailey's background. He hoped an impromptu plan wouldn't backfire. "Tell her you already have a high school diploma and that I pulled strings to get you to take part in the program because I didn't trust you to stay at my home with only the housekeeper looking after you. Then tell her she needn't worry about you being in the competition, because I'm not letting you. That was the deal we made. You'd sell caricatures and my paintings on the weekends here in Kerrville."

She looked at him with a tilted head. "That's so close to the truth that I can't tell the difference."

"Exactly. Never lie when you don't have to, and if you do, stretch the truth as little as possible." He looked at the students pulling ahead of them and pointed. "Catch up to them. Sometime this morning, move near Candice and tell her what we talked about. Don't press her too hard about her mother or where she might be. She'll tell you everything once she realizes you're not a threat. In fact, expect her to recruit you to help her win the competition."

"She's good and might not need any help."

"Everyone here is good. You included."

Her smile widened. "Yeah, but I'm the only one who gets personal instruction from the great Fen Maguire whenever I ask."

"You rarely ask."

She flipped her hair. "That's because I'm already very good. You said so yourself."

He had to admit she'd won this round, but it was only one of many. He tried to get in the last word by saying, "Keep your eyes and ears open. Lou will be in town within the hour to follow up and keep me informed."

"Do I tell Candice about Lou?"

"You and Lou are my secret agents. As things stand now, Candice is only interested in winning the competition. Let's not show any more of our hand than we have to. You need to make it clear to her you're not a threat to win the competition."

"But, I could be."

He shook his head. "I'm taking your name off the list of competitors. Besides, do you want to be well off financially or get your name and picture in the local paper?"

"Both."

"You can't have both this time around."

"I'll take the money."

"Good choice. Fame is fleeting and doesn't pay the bills."

"Speaking of... my SUV is making a grinding noise when I step on the brakes."

"It sounds like you need new pads and maybe the rotors turned or replaced. You're looking at five to six hundred bucks. It's a good thing we worked those fairs and festivals this spring."

She tilted her head back and rolled her eyes. "Forget the fame. I'm working weekends."

"This place has quite a reputation for artists and sculptors. People flock here in the summer to enjoy the river, the food, and the craft fairs. I've already planned to set up our booth for a couple of weeks after the competition."

"Why not this weekend?"

"I need to go home this coming weekend. Bills to pay and decisions to make about selling cattle and the crops."

Bailey's bottom lip stuck out as a sign of displeasure. "I thought that's why you have Sam as your foreman."

Fen watched as the students moved closer to the highway. "Sam can run the farm twice as good as I can, but he doesn't like to make the big decisions and he won't sign anything except charges at the farm and ranch supply. Don't worry, we'll have a financially satisfying summer and it will start by staying here two weeks after these classes are over. From here, we'll move on to Waco, then hit a lot of other places after that."

She rubbed her hands together as a sign of pleasure. "Always thinking ahead, aren't you?"

"Until something trips me up."

"Like what?"

"Something unexpected."

"Like a murder?"

"That would do it."

Chapter Five

Candice approached as soon as Fen finished his lunch. "This morning you said you'd treat us like we were in college. Did you mean it?"

He suspected she was up to something but didn't know what. "Within reason. This is a private church-owned university, so keep that in mind before you tell me what you want."

She pulled a lock of long, dark hair over her left ear. "I'm not wild about crowding into a van with all these people. Can we take our own cars to the park this afternoon?"

"Not everyone has their own transportation."

"So? Not everyone who goes to college has a car."

He shrugged. "That seems like a reasonable request."

"Listen up, people. There are advantages and disadvantages to working on-site or in a studio. After today you get to choose. For those who brought your own vehicles, you're not required to ride in the university van to the park. Like I told you earlier, I'm trusting you to make adult decisions. Just like this morning, I'll be around the park this afternoon to check on each of you and give you advice if you want it. After today, the van will be available to shuttle you downtown and bring you back here for lunch and supper."

"Can we ride with someone if we don't have a vehicle or ours needs new brakes?" asked Bailey.

Laughs came from several in the group. "That's up to you, Ms. Madison. I congratulate you on not wanting to be a menace on the roadways."

More laughter as he said, "Let's get to the park and complete your next three sketches."

He noticed Bailey approach Candice and talk low enough that he couldn't hear their conversation above the noise of chairs scraping, feet shuffling, and students talking about carpooling. Candice shook her head, but Bailey persisted. Candice cast her gaze toward him and narrowed her eyelids, apparently suspicious of what Bailey was saying. Then the two left together.

Fen concluded that Bailey was setting a trap of sorts, but Candice was a wary prey. His protégé would need to be clever as a mature fox to trick the child of such a manipulative mother. It was clear both beauties were two rabbits from the same warren.

Fen called Lou on his way to the park. "Are you checked in?"

"I'm here, slaving over a hot laptop. Anything new?"

"Not much. Candice believes her mother is playing a game to get publicity."

Lou took a few seconds to answer. "That makes sense in a twisted sort of way. Jewell adheres to the philosophy that any type of publicity is better than none. I think I'll come over and have a talk with Candice."

"Not yet," said Fen. "Bailey's working on her now. Wait until later this afternoon. We'll be at Louise Hays Park until five. Do you know where it is?"

"I picked up a city map in the lobby. Anything else?"

"Sorry, I've been playing art instructor and not murder investigator since I returned from the river this morning."

"You're slipping. A super-sleuth like you should be able to multitask. Call if Bailey comes up with anything juicy. I need more meat on the bones of each of these stories."

"Speaking of meat, there's a wonderful Mexican food restaurant in town. How about fajitas for supper?"

"Yum and double yum." She paused. "We're not pretending we don't know each other like the last case we worked?"

"If Jewell makes a dramatic appearance and the locals don't botch this morning's investigation, there won't be any sleuthing to do."

"I thought you were leaning toward it being a complicated case of mistaken identity."

"Leaning, yes. Bent over with confidence? No. Besides, Chuck made it clear the people pulling strings were interested because they thought today's victim was Jewell."

"I'll be at the park around four thirty. Until then, I'll try to make something out of almost nothing with these stories."

Fen's phone went silent.

He arrived at the park and it couldn't have been a more perfect day. Cotton-ball clouds inched across an azure sky. The temperature never hit mid-eighties and the wind only had ambition enough to emit an occasional puff of breeze. The lake was a mirror with only the occasional ripple caused by children throwing rocks. The sound of water flowing over the low-water dam gave the birds an accompaniment to their songs. In the distance, below the dam, he noticed the yellow police tape at the site he visited after dawn and reconsidered his thought about it being a perfect day.

A few anglers dotted the bank of the lake while couples

spread blankets under the trees. Several students piled out of the van and joined those who'd brought their own vehicles. He approached the gathering and lifted his arms like a bird taking flight. "Think perspective and story. Let your sketches talk to you. Remember what I told you this morning about those things? If you nail them, your painting will make patrons stop and stare. Choose the spots for your three sketches carefully. Your work should evoke feelings." He flapped his arms. "Away with you. Go create something people can't wait to buy."

Like a crowd exiting a movie, the students soon spread out with sketch pads in hand. Some paired with a fellow student but most went their own way. Creating works of art is a solitary endeavor, and these students fit the profile of introverts.

As Fen worked his way from one student to the next, he noticed a muscular man approach a bored-looking student named Patrice Brown. She dressed in all black and insisted everyone call her P.B. The man handed her a flier and walked to the next person. It seemed a little strange that a man who looked like his photo belonged on the cover of a fitness magazine was making rounds in a public park. He wore a sleeveless black undershirt, spandex shorts, and black low-quarter shoes. Quadriceps rippled from a hundred yards away.

The man then approached a shy student by the name of Holly. She was almost as pretty as Candice but hid her beauty behind a pair of glasses. The lenses reminded Fen of portholes on a small ship. It surprised him that the conversation between those two lasted longer than the man's previous encounters. It was time to guard the flock.

Conversation punctuated by laughter broke off as Fen approached. Holly took a step away from the man and one toward her instructor. "Mr. Maguire, come meet Mr. Shanks. He's a fitness instructor who offers early morning yoga classes here in the park."

"Weather permitting," said the man as he issued a toothy grin and extended a hand for Fen to shake. The grip was firm, measured to match Fen's even though there was no doubt he could have snapped bones if he'd chosen to do so.

"It's Roy Shanks. I'm opening a new gym in town that will include yoga, Pilates, and super-high intensity workouts. The daybreak yoga classes are free to anyone who wants a great way to start their day."

Fen returned Roy's friendly smile and patted his stomach. "Heaven knows I need to do something about this bulge and love handles, but a leg injury restricts my exercise. A recumbent bicycle is about the extent of my ability until I quit being such a wimp and get my knee replaced."

"Come to sunrise yoga classes. I can teach you some stretches that will strengthen your core. Get that core strong and recovery from surgery will be much easier." Roy then presented him with a flier.

Holly looked at Fen with pleading blue eyes. "I told Mr. Shanks I'd have to have your permission to leave campus that early." She rolled her eyes. "Mrs. Dillworth's orders." She moved on without hesitation. "I've already decided I'm going to paint the lake and not the river in front of the college. I have a car and can bring others. Please, Mr. Maguire?"

"What about breakfast?"

"Mom's always on me about watching my weight. A protein shake is all I'm supposed to have for breakfast. I'll need to stop by the grocery and pick up almond milk, but otherwise, I don't need anything else."

Fen rubbed his chin. "This sounds like something you need to talk to your parents about."

"It's just Mom and she'll be all for it."

"Still, you'll need to ask her, and it would be best if at least one other student was here with you."

Roy's smile widened. "Holly is my second commitment, and I'm just getting started."

Fen raised his hands in surrender. "I'm not your daddy, and I told you I'd treat you like an adult. Have fun. Who knows, I might show up if I can drag my lazy self out of bed in time."

He wasn't serious about yoga, but the advice to strengthen his core was something he needed to do.

The day progressed with Fen ambling through the park, checking the progress of students' sketches, and soaking in the day's beauty. At four o'clock, he noticed Bailey and Candice walking into the park from the parking lot. Where had they gone and what had they been up to? Only one way to find out.

He intercepted them and asked, "Have you completed the sketches?"

He'd caught Bailey as she was sucking what looked like a strawberry milkshake through a straw. She nodded while Candice said, "Bailey suggested we go to the other side of the lake to get a different perspective. I'm glad she did. Things look so different from there. There are no buildings in the background, only the lake and the park. We didn't see anyone else sketching from that side. That should give me a leg up on the competition."

"Did that perspective speak to you?"

Candice sputtered out a dismissive sound. "Mom and I are ahead of you, Mr. Maguire. We don't waste time allowing locations to speak to me. I'll be painting to please the judges, not myself. We did extensive research on each of them including you, but that was before I knew you wouldn't be judging. We know those three dinosaurs prefer oils over acrylics and aren't fans of impressionist or abstract works. Statistically, they're more likely to give first place to a feel-good painting that portrays peace, family, and dogs. A Fourth of July scene with plenty of flags and bunting should please them."

He nodded like he agreed with her, even though he believed each artist should master the basics and then develop his or her own style if they wanted to stand out.

A voice came from over his shoulder. "Candice, darling, it's never wise to give away your secrets."

Fen spun too fast. His torso twisted, but his right shoe caught in the dry grass. An audible snap came from the knee he should have had replaced years ago. Down he went.

Bailey was at his side when he opened his eyes. "I heard it pop. How bad is it this time?"

"Bad enough, but not nearly as bad as last time."

He looked up at a woman with an hourglass figure showing off dancer's legs in white shorts. She wore a summer blouse of pastels, a floppy hat, and sunglasses. When she leaned over, silky-black hair cascaded over each shoulder. "Oh, dear. It's that knee again. You really must be more careful, Mr. Maguire."

He smiled through the pain. "You must be Jewell. I've been expecting you. Please excuse me if I don't get up."

Chapter Six

There he was once again, looking up with pain shooting from his trick knee. Needing to find a tree to lean against before he could attempt to get up, Fen turned his head, hoping he wouldn't have to crawl very far. Behind him stood a pecan tree not more than a few yards away. By locking his knee, he could use his arms and his good left leg to scoot backward with a three-point crab-walk until he had a backstop.

He made it halfway before another concerned face looked down at him. He smiled up and said, "Hello, Holly. This is a trick I'm practicing to entertain the class." He grimaced as another pain shot up his leg. "You don't seem impressed."

"Are you all right?" Her eyes seemed bigger than they should have, probably because of the glasses.

Jewell's words didn't match her tone when she gushed, "Holly, dear, you're here. I wasn't sure you'd be up for this competition after another second-place finish last month."

"Hello, Mrs. Key. I like to think I'm gaining ground on Candice."

"Children and their fairy tales," said Jewell. "You're always so amusing."

Holly offered a smile of complete innocence. "I'm so glad to see you alive. We were all afraid it was you they found in the river this morning."

For the first time, Jewell took a step back. "I'm sure I don't know what you're talking about."

Fen took over. "They found a woman matching your description in the river shortly after dawn."

"Well," snapped Jewell, "it's obvious it wasn't me, and I highly doubt she looks like me."

Fen thought a little goading might be in order. "The chief of police used the word 'doppelgänger' to describe her resemblance to you. The authorities suspect foul play. There'll be a lot of people relieved to know you're alive and well."

Jewell looked down on him with a haughty smile. "As you can see, I'm very much alive. There's nothing like a weekend in Las Vegas to rejuvenate a person."

Fen nodded that he understood even though he didn't agree. His one and only visit to Vegas left him unimpressed with the neon city rising from the desert. Needing more information from Jewell he asked, "How long does it take to get from San Antonio to Vegas in a private jet?"

"It usually takes me half a bottle of champagne." She arched her eyebrows. "But it really depends on my travel companion. Sometimes I lose all track of time. Do you know what I mean?"

"I used to."

"That's right. You're now like me, free from the shackles of marriage." She squatted beside him and ran her finger along his shirt sleeve. "I understand you've taken yourself off the market. Please tell me it isn't so. There are so few interesting bachelors these days."

It was time to get his back against the tree so he only had to defend a frontal attack from this cougar. Everyone followed his backward movement as Holly asked, "Don't you need an ambulance?"

"Ice, anti-inflammatory pain pills, a knee brace, and a couple of days' rest are all I need. That's all the doctors ever do, except tell me I need a new knee."

Candice spoke next. "Mother and I read that a woman shot you when you were a highway patrolman. I think that's very romantic."

"Nonsense," said Jewell. "A six-carat diamond engagement ring is romantic. Of course, there are plenty of other things that could substitute for diamonds."

Fen made it to the tree with his right leg sticking straight out. He turned to Bailey. "Would you mind going to my truck and getting my leg brace? If I keep this thing straight, I should be able to hobble to the parking lot. My crutches are in the back."

"I'll be right back."

While Fen was speaking to Bailey, Jewell pulled Candice aside. Over the years, Fen had learned a skill that served him well. He could concentrate on two people talking at the same time. Even though Jewell spoke in soft tones, he picked up the conversation between mother and child.

"Darling," whispered Jewell, "how good of an artist is this Bailey girl?"

"Very good, but she's not in the competition. She's Mr. Maguire's protégé."

"How interesting."

"She's like a stray dog that showed up on Mr. Maguire's doorstep. He took her in and she lives in an apartment over his garage that has its own small studio. He's always there to give her pointers."

"Are you sure she's not in the competition?"

"He said she's not, and he's not one of the judges."

"You've been busy scoping out the competition. Good girl." She cast her gaze toward Bailey. "What happened to her hand?"

"Burned it in a trailer fire while she was living with an uncle. Someone murdered him and Mr. Maguire solved the case. She's right-hand dominant, so the burns don't affect her ability to paint."

"Good job, darling, but I'll still verify everything you said. That's another lesson you'll need to learn. I almost married a man who claimed to have millions. He owed millions."

When mother and daughter finished their conversation which wasn't as private as they thought, they returned to Fen and Holly under the tree. He opened up a new conversation with Jewell. "Your disappearance caused quite a stir in the press. The police will want to interview you as soon as they hear you're safe and in town."

She flipped her wrist as if she were shooing away a gnat. "That's the price I pay for notoriety, but it's really nobody's business where I go."

"Perhaps you could let your ex-husbands in on that."

"Those men," she said. "How quaint of them to take wedding vows so seriously. They're sweet, each in their own way, but they can be absolutely smothering. I can't blame the first two or three, but the last ones knew what I was like and didn't hesitate to marry me."

When Fen shifted, a shaft of pain shot up his leg. He grimaced and said, "Remind me not to do that again."

"Are you talking about getting married or moving your knee?"

Holly patted his hand. "Mr. Maguire, try not to move."

"How sweet," said Candice. "Holly's pretending to be a nurse."

Holly stuck her tongue out at her nemesis. It seemed clear the girls held no love for each other. Or was Candice performing for her mother?

Time to change the conversation. "Tell me, Jewell, would you prefer to speak to a reporter or the chief of police first?"

"Such an interesting question, Fen." She batted her eyelashes. It seemed so natural, but he wondered how long she'd sat in front of the mirror practicing facial expressions. Relaying messages without words seemed to be her forte.

"It's always dramatic when an officer in uniform stands in front of a microphone." She paused. "But considering the size of this town, I think a news crew out of San Antonio would have a greater impact."

"What about a person who used to be a top crime reporter in Dallas? I understand she's in town and has access to national and state news outlets."

She took her time answering. "Not bad, but video is my preference. That's what sells."

"She can handle the video too."

Bailey arrived back with the knee brace and Lou Cooper in tow. Fen looked up at Jewell and said, "Here she is now. Jewell, this is Lou Cooper, reporter extraordinaire. Lou, this is Jewell Key."

Lou nodded. An almost imperceptible raising of her eyebrows was all the acknowledgment she received from Jewell.

Bailey bent down and instructed Holly to ease Fen's leg off the ground while she slipped on the brace and cinched it tight. He gritted his teeth and said, "Good job, ladies. Let me rest a couple of minutes and I'll get up."

"Not before you take these three Advil tablets," said Lou.

Lou handed him a bottle of water and then began setting up a tripod with telescoping legs. She turned to Jewell. "I can get all the footage for the television stations and you won't have to wait on a crew from San Antonio to arrive. The light is perfect if we start now. Leave everything to me and you'll be on the six and ten o'clock news."

"Are you sure?" asked Jewell.

"I've been doing this for more years than I care to mention. This afternoon I wrote the bones of a story about you for publication. Now that you're no longer missing, it will be a breeze to add a few details."

Jewell seemed impressed by the sales pitch but needed clarification on one issue. "The police will hunt me down as soon as they find out I'm here. Can you get them arriving? It would be perfect if they arrive with lights and sirens."

Lou looked down at Fen. He gave a nod. "I have Chief Strange's number on my phone. When he hears that the stunning Jewell is here in the park with her amazing daughter, the artist prodigy Candice, he'll come like a greyhound chasing a mechanical rabbit. I'll advise him to come quick before the lady of mystery disappears again."

Jewell flashed a smile that matched her name. "That sounds scrumptious, Fen. You're not only an accomplished artist, you can turn a phrase with the best of them; and believe me, I've heard some wonderful phrases in my life. It's too bad you're not on the market. I think we could have fun."

"You wouldn't want me. I'm like a rusty old truck. You need a new sports car."

"Perhaps you're right."

He turned to Lou. "How much time do you need?"

"Ten minutes."

He held out his arms for Bailey and Holly to help him to his feet. "I'll call Ben Strange when I get to the parking lot."

Fen shifted his gaze to Jewell. "It's been a pleasure to see you again, Jewell. Your daughter has talent. I know with a mother like you she'll go far."

"She will," said Jewell. "I'll see to it."

After a long walk up a gentle incline, he leaned against the shaded side of his truck. He took a bandanna from his back pocket and wiped the sweat dripping from his chin. "Bailey, you're driving. I'll need you to get me some sort of ice pack along the way."

"You didn't bring one?"

"A major oversight on my part."

"It's a good thing Thelma put two in my suitcase. We had a bet you'd need them before we came home. I guess she won."

"Never bet against our housekeeper."

"I won't from now on."

"Do you want to release the lock on your brace so you can sit up front or leave it like it is and ride in the back seat of your truck?"

"Help me get in the back seat after I call the chief."

The chief picked up on the second ring. "Fen? Have you heard anything about Jewell? My phone is smoking from people demanding I find her."

"Better than that. I've been talking to her for the last fifteen minutes. She's expecting you to come talk to her at Hays Park. She's talking to a reporter now and requests you arrive with lights and siren. The reporter will film your approach."

"I'm sprinting to my SUV now. Ignore the panting if I get out of breath."

"Slow down. She's not going anywhere."

"Where's she been?"

"Vegas. Her disappearance was a publicity stunt to get recognition for her daughter."

"Does she have any idea how much manpower and money this has cost my department and agencies around the state?"

Fen cast his gaze toward Jewell. "Believe me, taxpayers' money is the last thing she cares about. Be careful; she's smart and almost too beautiful for words. She's building a career for her daughter and she'll stop at nothing. Cross her and there's a good chance you'll be looking for a new job."

"I understand what you're saying. The phone calls I received today were from people expecting me to stand at attention when I talked to them."

Fen had one more slice of advice for the chief. "Come in hot and make a good show for the camera. Tell her how worried the city was about her and how glad everyone in law enforcement is that she's safe. She'll take over from there and twist the story toward her daughter being in the art contest."

"I get it. No confrontation."

"Not unless you want to feel the claws of the biggest, baddest cougar you can imagine."

"Thanks for the advice. By the way, we have a positive ID on the woman in the river. It's Rose Cunningham, just like the license said. She's a widowed hairdresser from San Antonio. No kids. Her father made the ID at the morgue in San Antonio. She has a small tattoo on her lower back that was covered by her jeans when we saw her."

"Can you send me some photos of her?"

"She's on several dating sites. I'll send you the links."

"Do you still think she's a doppelgänger?"

"She is, and I think that's one of the coolest words I've ever heard. I can't stop using it."

"One more thing," said Fen. "You'll need to warn Jewell about the possibility she was the intended victim. Can you assign someone to watch her while she's in town?"

"It's tourist season. I'll be lucky if they don't fire me for scheduling too much overtime as it is. She has plenty of money. I'll recommend she hire bodyguards. That's the best I can do."

"Make sure you get that on tape with the reporter that's with her."

The sound of a siren came through Fen's phone. "I hear you coming."

"I need to let dispatch know what's going on and call a couple more units to respond. Might as well put on a good show and make the city fathers think I'm earning my keep."

The phone went dead. Bailey and Holly came and stood in front of him. Bailey asked, "Are you finished playing games with the cops?"

"All finished. I'll need you two to help me in and slide me to the far door."

"Duh. You act like I've never done this before. Holly's going to follow me to your condo. After we get you settled, she'll take me back to the university."

"I have a better idea," said Fen. "I won't be able to drive for several days. Find a repair shop and get your brakes fixed. You can use my truck."

"How will I know if it's a shop that won't cheat me or do a lousy job?"

"I have the number of the cop who took me to the river this morning. His name is Brent Craven, and he's lived here all his life. I'll call him for a referral."

Fen handed Bailey his crutches and said, "Okay, ladies, let's get me into the truck."

Several minutes later Bailey shut the back door of the truck and leaned against it to catch her breath. She looked at Holly who was also breathing hard and said, "Thanks for your help. Looks like I won't need a ride back to the university."

Holly shrugged. "I needed to stop by the store anyway. See you back on campus."

Bailey turned on the truck's air conditioning then watched the chief cross the bridge with his staccato light flickering, headlights flashing, and siren wailing. It wasn't long before another city officer arrived and came to an abrupt halt, leaving his emergency lights on but cutting off the siren.

It took longer to get to the condo than Fen expected because of the high number of tourists in town. He maneuvered his way from the truck to the elevator and into the condo. Bailey followed and went to the refrigerator's freezer as soon as they arrived. "You'll have to use real ice in plastic bags until I come back tonight with those blue things Thelma packed for you."

Fen was already in a recliner with the footrest up.

Bailey asked, "What are you going to do about supper?"

He shrugged. "Lou and I were supposed to go for Mexican food, but she now has stories to finish and sell. Once I take my prescription pain meds, I won't care about food. Which reminds me how far it is from this chair to the bathroom. Could you look in my shaving kit and get my happy pills?"

"You should eat first. I'll go get you something."

He shook his head. "There's a binder on the desk in the study with a restaurant guide. If you bring it to me, I'll find something."

"I'll order. You always get too much."

"You sound like Thelma."

"Uh... speaking of Thelma. It's a good thing this is a two-bedroom condo."

Fen's eyes opened wide. "What have you done?"

"She sort of called me while you were talking to the chief of police."

Fen groaned. "Tell me you didn't say anything about my knee."

"I didn't mean to. It was like she already knew."

His groan morphed into a mournful howl of a hound. "How could you do this to me?"

"It's not just you. She'll be up to her neck in my life too. I wouldn't put it past her to barge into my dorm room to make sure I'm not out partying."

"It would serve you right." He puffed out his cheeks. "I wouldn't trade Thelma for the world but having her around isn't my idea of a peaceful working vacation."

Bailey nodded in agreement. "You'd better heal quick this time, for both our sakes."

Chapter Seven

Instead of taking a couple of his high-powered pain pills immediately, Fen and Bailey agreed he'd wait and take them on a full stomach. They discarded the idea of Mexican food, as Bailey had her taste buds set on pizza. She called in an order for a large Meat Lover's and two salads. Claiming a shortage of drivers, delivery time was estimated at an hour and a half. Bailey decided to pick up the order after they promised it would be ready in fifteen minutes.

With a small, plastic bag full of ice resting on his knee and ibuprofen in his system, the pain wasn't unbearable as long as he kept still.

A knock sounded on the door five minutes after Bailey left. He hoped she hadn't locked it behind her, as he dreaded having to get out of the chair and walk. Only one way to find out. He hollered, "Come in." To his great relief, the sound of the door opening reached his ears.

"Nice condo," said Lou as she breezed in. "No time to waste. Where can I set up to edit the video and finish my story?"

He pointed to the office. "They taped the Wi-Fi password to the desk lamp. Knock yourself out."

She stopped at the office door and turned. "Anything new I need to know about before I contact the television stations?"

"Yeah. Bailey's on her way to pick up pizza. Are you hungry?"

"Starving. Call her and get me a Supreme. Make it a large so you'll have leftovers. You don't look like you'll be leaving for several days."

The office door closed behind her before he could respond.

It was almost an hour later when Lou emerged from the office. "Isn't Bailey back yet? My stomach thinks I'm fasting. It's not a bad idea, but I do my best writing when I'm munching on something."

"Did you get all your stories submitted and sold?"

"Yes, and not yet. The television stations are going to show it. The newspaper editors are working it into their next editions. They'll need to cut the word count to fit the space, but several will publish the story tomorrow. I'm not so confident about anything national or even the Dallas or Houston markets. If the body in the river was Jewell's, the story would have a wider audience."

"Let's hope that doesn't come to pass."

His comment got her attention. She sat on the edge of the couch near him. "Are you still thinking this was a case of mistaken identity?"

He cast his gaze to the sliding glass door, which opened to the patio. "There's no evidence at this point to back up that theory."

"That's not what I asked."

He brought his gaze back to her. "I don't have a good feeling about Jewell after seeing the woman in the river. My opinion of Jewell may cloud my judgment about her being the intended victim. She's easy to dislike. I keep thinking, if I can't stand her, how much more would a spurned ex-husband or lover have against her?"

Lou settled back into the couch. "You may be onto something concerning motive. My research shows she went into each marriage intending to divorce her husbands. Divorce settlements are how she made her millions."

Fen put the pieces together. "That makes perfect sense if you can twist your mind that tight. I bet she used some excellent attorneys who advised her how to do things that would optimize her settlements."

Lou smiled and said, "Keep talking. You're on the right track. What do you think she did?"

He looked up at the ceiling. "No prenuptial agreements and joint bank accounts to start with. Have the victim, er, the husband, sign over stock, bonds, and partial ownership of businesses. I can also see her expecting expensive gifts; I bet she has quite a collection of jewelry. I bet she also talked those five men into purchasing trophy homes. She'd get half the value of them but wouldn't agree to sell until they appreciated."

"Well done," said Lou. "Except you left out gold bars and Bitcoin. She also has an affinity for yachts. So far, she's cashed in on two of them. A third is currently for sale."

He added, "All the while I'll bet she did things to put the husbands in compromising situations and lined up witnesses to testify against them if they didn't agree to her terms."

Lou raised her right hand. "The crazy thing is, several of them would take her back..." She snapped her fingers. "...that fast." She shrugged. "I don't get it. I tried three times and couldn't hold any of my husbands' interest more than a few years. I was lucky to get a Snickers bar on Valentine's Day."

Fen looked again at the patio door. "Never underestimate the persuasive ability of a beautiful woman. Mix that with a devious mind and you'd better hold on tight to your heart and your wallet."

"You don't know how lucky you were that you snagged a good woman," said Lou.

Fen swallowed hard.

Lou then asked a question that was vexing him. "Do you think Jewell is in danger?"

"I discussed it with Chief Strange. He doesn't have the staff to assign anyone to watch her. We agreed he'd suggest she hire bodyguards."

Lou leaned forward. "I got him explaining that to her on tape. She thanked him for his concern and said she'd consider it."

It seemed as if Lou didn't finish her thought, so he asked, "So? What else did she say?"

"Nothing, but I could tell she wadded up the suggestion of bodyguards and threw it away."

"Doesn't surprise me. I'm not sure I've ever met anyone so self-absorbed and sure they have the world by the tail."

A knock on the door interrupted any further discussion. Lou rose while Fen resettled the ice pack on his knee. From behind him he heard, "Sorry to interrupt. How's the patient?"

"Come in, Chief Strange."

"Call me Ben. It's after five o'clock and no one else is around."

The two walked into his field of vision. "Hello, Chief. Have a seat. Are you finished with your fifteen minutes of fame?"

"More like ninety seconds, and that's before they edit. As gorgeous as Jewell and her daughter are, I'm under no illusion that anyone will want to see my ugly mug."

Fen chuckled. "The older I get, the more I realize my face is better suited for radio than television." He took a breath.

"Lou was telling me Jewell isn't keen about the idea of hiring bodyguards."

The chief's head shook. "I tried talking to her again, but she shut me down before I could complete my second sales pitch."

"A fool and their health are soon parted."

Lou rolled her eyes. "You and your butchered proverbs."

It was time to ask a serious question. Fen looked at the chief. "Is there anything new related to Rose Cunningham's death?"

Ben nodded, then looked at Lou. "I'm sorry, but what I'm about to say has to be off the record."

Lou huffed. "Do you have any idea how much I hate it when people like you tell me that? Ninety-nine percent of the time, it doesn't make a hill of beans difference when the public knows whatever it is you think is so important. I'll have you know that the press serves a vital function in society, and—"

"Lou," snapped Fen. "Play nice. You've already had an exclusive dropped in your lap as a present. Besides, you haven't even heard Ben's reasons."

She bit her lower lip to stem the flow of words.

Ben raised his eyebrows. "Would it make you any happier if I gave you an hour's notice before I issued a press release?"

"Two hours would be better."

Fen frowned and narrowed his gaze with what he hoped would be a look that communicated disapproval.

"Oh, all right," said Lou. "What's the big news?"

"Again," said Ben. "No release until it's official. The DA has an arrest warrant on his desk, ready for his signature. All he's waiting on is the ruling from the coroner that Rose Cunningham's death is a homicide."

A name shot from Fen's mouth. "Ray-Ray?"

"Who's Ray-Ray?" asked Lou.

Ben answered. "Raymond Ray, a street musician, vagrant, and habitual substance abuser."

"Evidence?" asked Fen.

"When he finally sobered up enough this afternoon, he couldn't explain how he came to be in possession of Rose Cunningham's credit cards and over two hundred dollars in cash. He'd already admitted he only earned enough playing and singing to buy three bottles of wine and a couple of downers. Said he'd been having trouble sleeping lately."

"What do you think?" asked Fen.

Ben shrugged. "I'm not sure it matters much what I think. The DA and mayor believe there's more than enough for an arrest. The mayor wants it in the press as soon as possible to show how efficient the city's police force is."

"They're right about there being plenty of evidence for an arrest," said Fen. "I guess you'll have to wait on forensics to see if there's any exculpatory evidence that could clear Ray-Ray."

Lou added, "My experience with small Texas towns is that DAs and public officials like quick, simple convictions. Are you being pressured to get a confession out of Mr. Ray?"

He smiled. "You know I can't comment on an ongoing investigation."

Fen chuckled. "How many times have I used that line?"

The door swung open behind him. Bailey came into his peripheral vision, headed to the kitchen. The smell of pizza drifted to him and awakened his gnawing hunger. "You wouldn't believe the crowds in town. Ordering the second pizza took forever. It baffled that poor girl taking my order that I needed to add another pizza to an existing order. I finally told the girl to ring up the orders separately." She handed Fen the receipts.

"Good girl," said Lou. "You learned something from that business class you took."

"I learned simple transactions like that a long time before I took Business 101. Cancel the first order on the Point-of-Sale monitor, put everything on a separate order, run the card, and hand over the food."

She brought plates down from a cabinet. "Come and get it while it's still sort of hot."

Fen said, "That means you, too, Ben."

He rose. "I need to get home. If I come home smelling like pizza, Julie'll put me on a diet of raw carrots and broccoli. Thanks for all your help. It looks like all the concern for Jewell was a waste of time."

When the front door closed behind Ben, Lou gave Fen a sideways look. "Do you think he's right?"

Fen didn't think so but had nothing to go on but a gut feeling. Instead of answering Lou's question, he spoke louder than necessary so Bailey could hear him in the kitchen. "I'll start with a slice of each."

Lou rose and spoke as she walked to the kitchen. "I've been around you long enough to know I need to stay in town a while longer when you don't answer a question like the one I just asked."

Chapter Eight

Talk ceased until everyone had polished off a portion of their meal. Fen looked at Bailey, who was halfway through her second slice. "I noticed there's a bit of friction between Candice and Holly. What's the story behind that?"

"It's not just Candice and Holly but between their moms too. It seems both girls go to the same private prep school in San Antonio. Some sort of academy. Very hoity-toity. Candice doesn't hold back on telling everyone how exclusive it is. Holly isn't as bad, but behind those enormous glasses there's a girl who's tired of finishing in second place."

"Holly's parents must be well off too."

Lou jumped into the conversation even though she had to squirrel a bite of pizza into the side of her mouth to talk. "Holly's mom is single. Her name is Cindi Gilmore. Never married and no birth announcement for Holly that I could find." She chewed the bite and swallowed. "Cindi's father owns a string of state banks. It's said he has a Midas touch when backing real estate ventures. There are seven branch offices in a rough triangle, from Austin to San Antonio to

Kerrville. He was in on the ground floor of the real estate boom."

"Why did you do research on Cindi?" asked Fen.

"I followed a thread on the Internet. Search for Jewell and you'll soon find Candice. Follow the stories of Candice's life, and there's Holly. That led me to search for Holly's mother, Cindi. It was probably a long chase down a rabbit hole but I'm used to gathering information I'll never use."

Bailey shifted her gaze from Lou. "Didn't you meet Mrs. Gilmore when she helped Holly move into the dorm?"

"I had no chance to talk to any of the parents other than Jewell. She wanted to make sure I knew what a special artist Candice is. That's when they had me scheduled to be a judge. After she bent my ear for an hour, I made myself scarce and bowed out of judging. The other three judges understood and said they'd try to look out for Jewell."

Lou picked up a glass of Diet Coke but didn't raise it to her lips. "There's no telling what Jewell is doing to make sure Candice wins again. If faking her disappearance is a preview, this may be an interesting two weeks."

By this time Bailey had taken another bite. She held up a single finger as a sign she had something else to say. "That's why Candice spent so much time with me today. Her mom sent her on a mission to verify Fen wouldn't judge. I think I convinced her you weren't, but she didn't buy that you wouldn't have an influence on the outcome. Expect a cougar attack once you're back on your feet."

Fen groaned as Lou chuckled.

Wanting to change the course of the conversation, Fen asked. "Did you get either Candice or Holly to tell you what things Jewell has done to make sure Candice wins?"

"I tried with Candice but she was tight as an oyster. I think her mother coached her to never discuss it. Holly's a different story. If half of what she said is true, and I think it is, you might as well take the first-place trophy to the engravers and put Candice's name on it."

"You did everything but answer my question. What things?"

Bailey tilted her head and gave him a look that communicated he should already know. "Do I have to spell it out for you? She reads people, finds their weak spot, and then exploits it. For men, she's a walking, talking, flirting fantasy. She can bat those long lashes over her violet eyes and make most guys want to do anything to please her. For others, she's smart, or should I say crafty? Finally, she's ruthless. It's the usual bag of tricks: political or social pressure from well-connected people. If she has to she'll resort to bribery. Holly swears Candice's mother uses private detectives to find dirt on the judges in every competition. She makes sure Candice wins, no matter the cost."

Fen and Lou traded glances. He spoke what he thought they both were thinking. "You know way too much for someone only eighteen years old."

Bailey grinned. "I'll take that as a compliment. Candice thought it was cool that I know how to hotwire cars and pick locks. She wants me to teach her." She held up her hand. "Don't worry. I told her those days were over."

The trio went back to their meals. Jewell's obsession with her daughter occupied Fen's mind, along with his throbbing leg. By now the Supreme was barely warm and the Meat Lover's had cooled to room temperature. He looked at the slice in his hand and put it back on his plate.

The knock on the condo's door brought attention to something besides food, Jewell, and Candice. Bailey sprung from her seat to answer it. Fen closed his eyes as a voice boomed from behind him. "What kind of town is this? I haven't seen so many cars crammed into a city in my life. Are they giving something away?"

Bailey didn't take the bait. "Hi, Thelma. Do you have more bags to bring up?"

"Sure do. I bought enough food for a week. You can forget about that nasty food they serve at college. I'll put some meat on those skinny bones of yours if it's the last thing I do."

Thelma rounded his chair and scowled down at him like he was a puppy who hadn't made it outside in time. "You did it again, didn't you? I told Sam the day you left, I said, 'Sam, that man will not wear his brace like I told him to, and he's gonna' end up two hundred miles from home and not be able to move.'"

"It's not two hundred miles, Thelma."

She gave him her best squint-eyed look of displeasure. "Might as well have been a thousand for all the traffic out on the roads. When did they raise the speed limit to a hundred and forty? People passed me like I was riding a mule, not driving my truck." She looked down. "Where's the ice packs I sent with Miss Bailey?"

Bailey spoke as quickly as she could. "I came here straight from the park when Mr. Fen wrenched his knee and we had to improvise with a plastic garbage bag. Someone had to go get supper for this crew, so I haven't been back to the university to get them."

"You did good, Miss Bailey. No need for you to make an extra trip. I brought four more of the blue slushy things that go in the freezer. It's always good to come prepared."

Thelma cast her gaze to Lou, who had retreated to the kitchen. "Were you with him when he went down?"

"No, ma'am. I didn't get to the park until after he'd twisted his knee again."

Fen took a chance and entered the one-sided conversation. "It's not near as bad as the last time."

Thelma jerked her head back to stare at him. "Don't remind me of the last time. There you were having to hobble up the steps of a stinky, old apartment in Nacogdoches with that worthless leg doing nothing but gettin' in the way. And to top it off you didn't call me for help."

"It was a one-bedroom," said Fen with a plea for understanding in his voice.

"Don't matter. Miss Sally, rest her soul, made me promise I'd take care of you. You made me feel like I failed her." She looked at the half-eaten piece of pizza on his plate resting on the end table beside him. "And here you are eating nasty pizza with crust that tastes like a piece of cardboard."

Fen had to admit that the pizza was sitting heavy on his stomach, but this wasn't the time for a public confession. He shifted in his chair and a spasm of pain hit him.

"Why'd you just yelp like a pup with his tail stepped on? Didn't you take any of those high-powered pills the doctor gave you?"

"Not yet. I wanted to get something on my stomach and we had things to discuss concerning a case."

"What case?"

"We thought there might be a murder case to solve, but the local police have a suspect in custody."

"And how were you planning on solving anything by sitting in that chair?"

"I was on both feet, doing fine. Then the police found a woman's body in the river." He pulled a hand down the side of his face. "Wait. Before that, a woman who looked just like the woman in the river disappeared and—"

Thelma held up both hands like an overzealous traffic cop. "You're not making a lick of sense and I don't want to hear any more about it." She turned to Bailey. "Go find his pain pills." She then turned to Lou. "Do you have time to help me tote things up from the parking garage?"

"Sure. Then I can clean up the kitchen."

Thelma tilted her head. "From the moment I walked through that door, the kitchen became my responsibility. You're welcome to come for meals three times a day, but I'll thank you for staying out of the kitchen."

Lou gave her head an exaggerated nod. "Understood."

Fen asked, "Thelma, where did you park?"

"First open spot I found. Close to the elevator."

"You'll need to park next to my truck. Each condo has two assigned parking places. They'll tow your truck if you park in the wrong spot."

Thelma shook her head. "Taking someone else's truck sounds like a good way to get shot."

Fen added, "Bailey needs to get back to campus. She'll take my truck until my leg is good enough for me to drive."

Bailey came with his pills. He unscrewed the cap and took two. Bailey said, "I thought you were supposed to only take one?"

He winked at her. As much as he loved Thelma, he wasn't about to listen to her rattle off complaints for the rest of the evening. One pill made him woozy. Two, and an earthquake couldn't wake him. He'd be on his feet again in two or three days and Thelma would have no reason to stay. Of course that didn't mean she wouldn't make up an excuse to prolong the visit.

Fen caught Bailey by the hand. "Thanks for all you're doing. There's one more thing. Tell the students I might show up any time and they need to do their absolute best on their projects. Until then, work with them the best you can."

"Do you want me to make the rounds of the art studio, the river, and the park?"

"Please. That should help convince all the students and their parents that you're not competing, just in case there are lingering doubts."

"I'm finishing a couple of paintings from East Texas. I can't wait until the competition is over and we can set up a booth in town."

"Go ahead and set up this weekend. You may have to get a permit. Get Brent Craven's phone number off my phone. When you call him about getting your SUV in the shop for brakes, ask him about the permit. He'll know what to do."

She smiled at him. "I may practice some of Jewell's techniques and get him to help me set up the booth too."

Fen groaned again.

Chapter Nine

F en cracked open an eye. The only light in the room came from the clock on the nightstand, which read 6:57. He wondered if it was morning or night. With the room's high quality blackout curtains, it was hard to tell. Could he have possibly slept a full day? A vague memory of Thelma guiding him to bed came. It was still daylight then, and being June, that meant he went to bed before sundown. There were snatches of images of her putting ice packs on his knee. Was it once or twice? He blinked himself awake and concluded it was morning. Even a double dose of painkillers wouldn't knock him out for twenty-four hours. Or did they?

His door opened before he could throw the covers back, and light flooded into the room.

"Don't you try to get up without your crutches." Before he reached down, Thelma handed them to him and was pulling back his covers. "Don't you be falling in the bathroom either. The last time that happened, you wedged yourself between the toilet and the cabinet and I thought we'd have to tear the sink out to get you out of there. When you're finished, get back in bed. I'll bring your breakfast to you."

When Thelma was barking orders, it was safer to nod or shake your head than answer her. Fen nodded, pulled himself up with the aid of his crutches, and walked to the bathroom, putting no weight on his right leg.

He spoke as he walked, "I don't remember putting on these pajama pants."

"That's because you took two of those feel-good pills. I barely got you out of the recliner before you went limp as an old sock."

Fen grimaced. It was times like this that made him thankful he wasn't given to modesty.

He emerged from the bathroom with face washed, teeth brushed, and no stabs of pain from his knee, only a dull ache. He'd lived with the unstable knee for so long, he could tell by the loudness of the pop how long he'd be out of commission. This one had sounded like a two-day pop. He'd take strong pain killers for two days only. By using the crutches he could be back at the college tomorrow, if he could convince Thelma. He'd need to come up with something original to appease her, which would take some thinking.

Before and after breakfast, Thelma applied fresh ice packs. He took another pain pill and it wasn't long before he slipped into that half-awake, half-asleep state. He looked forward to this state of consciousness and dreaded it at the same time. If he dreamed of his former wife, it was as if Sally was with him again. All was well with their world, and his level of contentment reached its peak. At other times, bad dreams filled with images of suffering and death would come with the same clarity of colors. They left him thrashing the bed sheets and soaked in sweat. One last type of dream sometimes visited in his half-awake state. They made no sense at all, just images of completely random scenes.

He concluded a long time ago that his dreams reflected his life. Sometimes things were wonderful. Other times events and people around him were evil. Finally, there was a lot that made little or no sense.

Without warning the image of Rose Cunningham lying face down in the Guadalupe River popped into his mind. He wondered if he should do more to investigate her death. Did the police really have the right man in custody? What about Jewell? Was she the intended victim? Was it his place to try harder to convince her to seek protection? He felt the effects of the pill and slipped out of one state of consciousness into another. Sally came back for a visit. He settled against the pillows content as a kitten after lapping a bowl of cream.

By the time Bailey arrived at six in the evening, he'd slept off the effects of the medication and Sally had retreated, leaving him alone again. Smarter people than him might make sense of the recurring dream, but not him. It was time to focus on the here and now.

"You look much better," said Bailey as she flopped on the couch.

"I feel better. I'm swearing off the hard stuff and going to over-the-counter pain relievers. Thelma should receive a medal for keeping my knee iced, even when I slept."

From the kitchen came a voice. "Twenty minutes on, and twenty minutes off. That and DMSO."

Bailey scrunched up her nose. "What's DMSO?"

"Horse lineament," said Thelma. "It's something that cures a bunch of things."

Fen explained, "I use it as a topical anti-inflammatory, but you can get it in pill form, too."

"You'd heal faster if you used the same stuff Sam puts on his horse."

He lowered his voice, but not enough. "Sam picks his up at the feed store but it's not approved for humans. I use an approved version of cream that I order online."

"You're stubborn as a mule. That qualifies you for the stuff Sam uses," said Thelma.

Bailey laughed at the quick comeback. He needed to change the topic. "How did things go with the students today?"

Bailey stood and stretched. "It started early. Several of us went to the daybreak yoga classes."

"You went?" asked Fen.

"I found out last night that Candice signed up after she heard Holly was going. I thought it best I make sure those two didn't tear into each other."

"Any problems?"

Bailey reached down, touched her toes, and kept talking as she placed her palms on the carpet. "They came in their own cars and set up their mats with several other people between them. I could tell they were keeping tabs on each other. Holly stayed after class, talking to the instructor. It looked to me like they called a truce since neither mother was around."

"How many students went?"

"Five... no, six. If you count me, there were seven. The same number of adults, but I think that number will grow."

Fen examined a small hole in one of his white socks. With his foot elevated on the footrest of the recliner, he couldn't help but notice it. "What makes you say there'll be more people coming?"

"Adult women," said Bailey. "The instructor is quite a hunk for a guy that looks to be a few years shy of forty. His spandex shorts were a hot topic of discussion among the ladies I walked behind on my way back to the parking lot. Several of them said they were inviting friends to join them tomorrow."

"Nothing like lust to start your day off," joked Fen.

"Listen to you in there," said Thelma. "Jealous of that man because his chest hasn't dropped over his belt." She paused. "What's this feller's name, Bailey? I may need to check him out."

"Roy is what he wants everyone to call him. I don't remember his last name."

Fen remembered it being Roy Shanks, but it wasn't worth mentioning. He asked, "What other news do you have for me?"

"I called Brent Craven. He gave me the name of the repair shop he uses. He even followed me there and brought me back to campus. Nice guy, but you're right, he could do with a regular diet of Thelma's cooking."

"The shop could take you in on such short notice?"

"They had a cancellation, so I left my SUV and they'll get to it first thing in the morning."

"Did you ask about a vendor's permit for this weekend?"

"Brent is meeting me at lunch tomorrow at city hall. He said they tell people they have to take the application and bring it back later, but with him along, I'll be in and out in fifteen minutes with a permit in hand."

"Let me guess. Officer Craven has time to help you set up our booth on Saturday."

Bailey grinned. "He couldn't guarantee helping to take it down, but he'll help with setup." She pointed to the television set. "Have you seen tomorrow's weather forecast?"

Thelma arrived with a glass of tea for each of them. "Clear tomorrow morning, giving way to showers and thunderstorms in the afternoon."

"Thanks for the tea," said Fen. "Bailey, get word to the students tonight that they can paint in any of the three locations tomorrow morning, but I want everyone in the university art studio tomorrow afternoon. I'll be there to check the progress of their paintings."

It didn't surprise him that Thelma had placed her hands on her hips and was winding up to give him an enormous piece of her mind. He raised the volume of his voice. "What I meant to say is that Thelma and I will be there tomorrow afternoon to give them a lesson in sales. They'll need to bring their sketches. While I'm sitting with my leg propped up with ice packs on it, Thelma will play the role of a prospective buyer."

Bailey shook her head. "But they're just getting started on their paintings."

"I'll review their paintings first. Then they'll pretend Thelma's a customer who's commissioned a work and she'll select what she thinks is the most promising scene of the six. This will teach them the difference between pleasing themselves and pleasing a customer."

Thelma stood with her mouth hinged open. "I don't know a thing about art."

"That's not the point. Most customers don't either. This will be the student's lesson in sales, not style. You'll be doing them, and me, a tremendous favor. All you have to do is be yourself, tell them what you think, and select the sketch you'd most like to see in a painting. I'll be sitting right beside you if any of them pop off. With you there, I'm sure I won't do anything foolish with my knee."

Bailey's grin parted her lips. "You'll do great, Thelma. Just pretend Fen brought you several sketches and asked what you thought of them."

Thelma wrung her hands. "I'd better bake a bunch of cookies. My honest opinions tend to rub people the wrong way. With cookies, at least they'll leave with one good taste in their mouth."

Chapter Ten

Fen wanted to go onto the patio and watch the day come alive while he sipped his second cup of coffee. Longing to get some fresh air, he picked up his crutches and moved from the chair to the sliding glass door.

Thelma was out of the kitchen before he could flip the lock. "There's not a footstool out there so you'd best get back in that recliner. I'll bring you a fresh ice pack."

Confined to the recliner, he proposed his first compromise of the day to the overly observant cook and housekeeper. "If I can't go outside, let's at least open the patio door and listen to the birds. A little fresh air would be nice."

"You sit. I'll do all the opening and closing."

It was a decent compromise. Not his best effort but he knew he couldn't talk her into moving the recliner outside.

Halfway through his coffee, the ringing of his phone caught him with eyes closed, taking in the smells and sounds of the river. Bailey's name and photo appeared on the screen. "Good morning. How was yoga today?"

"A bit of a stretch." The laugh that followed sounded like a young woman enjoying a carefree day.

He groaned at her attempt at humor. "Did you see that printed on a shirt?"

"No, but Roy had something on today that made everyone in the class laugh. He wore another of those muscle-man shirts that read, *I flexed and the sleeves fell off.*"

It was Fen's turn to laugh, which he did with gusto. "I bet the ladies liked that."

"Jewell seemed to."

"That's a surprise. I didn't have her pictured as a woman who'd wake up early enough to catch a sunrise workout. Did Candice have anything to say about her mother coming to check out the local talent?" He heard Bailey close the door to his truck.

"Candice and her mom did yoga side by side. Jewell must do it every day. She can twist into more shapes than those plastic-coated wires that come on loaves of bread. Candice is very good too. Roy took turns staring at both of them. He also spent a lot of time looking at Holly. If it weren't for the glasses, she'd be H-O-T, hot. Just as attractive as Jewell and Candice."

Fen whispered, "I'm not sure the world could stand two more Jewells."

"What's that supposed to mean?"

"Nothing. Forget I said it." He needed to change the subject. "Any trouble between Candice and Holly?"

"Not today. At least not yet. Holly picked a spot far away from Jewell and Candice, who made sure they were right in front of Roy. Holly came early and was talking to Roy when I got there, but he moved on pretty quick. After the class, it was a little weird. Holly rolled up her mat and ran to her car after the session."

"Was she upset?"

"I couldn't tell. She might have been mad or upset about something. You never know with girls that age. Anything can set them off."

He considered telling her some students were only a few months younger than her, but didn't want to spar with both her and Thelma on the same morning. "Anything else?"

"Candice and her mom made another enemy this morning."

"Oh? Who?"

"P.B. Brown."

"Patrice? Our girl in black? What did they do to her?"

"They repeatedly called her Patrice instead of P.B., even after she corrected them. She has daggers for eyes and a tongue that's sharp as any switchblade I ever carried."

"Point taken." He chuckled. "Get it? Point taken? Switchblade?"

"Quit while you're behind. My pun was much better."

He wasn't ready to concede but this was getting them nowhere. "Tell me what Jewell and Candice did to P.B."

"The queen of goth had already rolled out her mat on the front row, directly in front of Roy. Jewell started a conversation with P.B. and got her positioned to where P.B. couldn't see her mat. Candice moved it to the second row. That left Mrs. Key and Candice front row, center stage. I didn't hear what P.B. said to them, but it ended with P.B. picking up her mat and storming off while Jewell and Candice laughed at her."

"Did Roy say anything?"

"He was busy introducing himself to the new ladies who showed up. As soon as the class ended, Jewell wanted to know about his new gym and the programs he offered." She paused. "I don't get it. Jewell was practically throwing herself at him, but from what you've told me, she trolls for much bigger fish than a guy trying to make a living running a local gym."

How could he explain Jewell to her so she could understand the hunting tactics of a cougar? He took his best stab at it. "People surprise you with what they do and don't do. Perhaps Jewell finds Roy attractive. Who knows, she might be tired of catching big fish and wants to catch and release a few little ones. It could be she likes the attention. I'm sure a good psychologist could give you a dozen more reasons."

He could almost see Bailey shaking her head as she said, "There's no doubt Jewell lives on attention, but she gets that all the time. I like the catch and release little fish answer. You know, just to keep in practice."

It occurred to him the eighteen-year-old may have a better read of Jewell than he did. Time to change subjects. "Did anything happen in the dorm last night?"

"Nothing bad. Someone had the bright idea to paint each others' toenails as a way of getting to know one another. Holly painted mine and put little gnomes on them. I did hers with miniature horses. Ever try to fit a horse on the nail of the little toe? I should have done daises." She paused. "We were good last night, but give us a couple more days. Groups and cliques are forming. They'll find trouble to get into."

"That reminds me," said Fen. "If you get into trouble, you'll get a roommate named Thelma. I've already cleared it with Mrs. Dillworth."

The phone went dead. "Checkmate," he said.

Almost immediately his phone rang again. He thought it was Bailey calling with a comeback to the idea of Thelma invading her life. The caller ID said otherwise. He swiped the green circle and said, "Good morning, Lou."

"Have you had your time with Sally yet? I didn't want to interrupt you."

"I've been up for quite a while." He paused. "I'm using the word *up* loosely."

"Are you ambulatory?"

"Dr. Thelma says I need to stay in the recliner or in bed for two more days. There's no way I can be out that long, so we reached a compromise. She's driving me to the university this afternoon and helping me with the students."

Thelma raised her voice enough to be heard in any room of the condo. "I heard that. I still don't think that's a good idea. Don't you remember the last time you tried to get on your feet too soon?"

Lou whispered into the phone. "I'd come over and tell you a few things, but I don't want to interfere with your morning with Thelma."

"I heard that, too!"

"Wow! That woman has ears like a bat."

"No secrets in my house," said Fen. "What's new in the news?"

"Two of Jewell's ex-husbands got into a dust-up last night in the bar of the Y.O. Hotel. That's where I'm staying."

"I didn't know any of her exes were in town."

"Some fools never learn. From what the bartender told me, they acted like a couple of high school football studs chasing the head cheerleader."

He finished a quick sip of coffee and asked, "Which ex-husbands, and was there any bloodshed?"

"I'll answer the last question first. A little blood, and the cops came and told them to go to their rooms to cool off. Jeremy Key was one of them."

Fen picked up on the last name. "He must be Candice's father."

"Correct. Jeremy is husband number one. Jewell fleeced him and moved on to her next victim, who is Cliff Rouse, the second stop on her way to financial independence. All three are here at the Y.O."

He dragged his hand over the stubble on his chin and spoke words not intended for anyone in particular. "She must cast a wicked spell over men."

"Amazing, isn't it? After all these years and they're still fighting to get her back."

"From what I gleaned from you, all five would take her back."

Fen had to wait as a squadron of motorcycles moved down the street in front of the condos. Once the thundering metal steeds passed, he asked, "Were you in the bar when Jeremy Key and Cliff Rouse locked horns?"

"I was pumping the bartender for information on local events, points of interest for tourists, and anything else I can use to cobble together stories that I can sell to newspapers or magazines. This little town is jumping with tourists and has some interesting history, but I'd rather write stories about you solving another murder." She let out a sigh. "No such luck. With Raymond Ray still in jail for killing Rose Cunningham and Jewell back from her publicity stunt, I've resorted to befriending bartenders for leads."

He considered her words. "My mind's still a little fuzzy. You mentioned Rose Cunningham. I still think there's more to her death than what the locals believe."

"Are you still preaching that it's a case of mistaken identity?"

He didn't want to build a case on nothing more than a gut feeling, but the unease wouldn't go away. "If you run out of things to do, dig deeper into Ray-Ray's past. What was he like before he soaked up too much wine and pills?"

"I'll see what I can do." Lou paused. "Don't get mad at me for asking, but are you reliving the time you discovered the sheriff falsely convicted Sam and you got him out of prison?"

"Thanks to the pain pills, my mind isn't sharp enough to

think that deep. You may be right about me projecting an experience onto Rose's murder, but you can't believe what an uphill battle it is to prove someone's innocence after they're convicted and sentenced."

"If you're right that will juice up the story. I'll also try to find out more about Rose Cunningham." She paused. "Are you sure that gimpy leg is good enough for you to leave the condo this afternoon?"

"The classes and competition only last two weeks and I've already missed a day and a half. Between the brace, crutches, and Thelma watching me like an eagle, I'll be all right."

Thelma's voice rang out. "You can forget about me picking you up if you fall."

Chapter Eleven

Thelma didn't scare easily but the drive into the university with its stately buildings standing tall and strong had her wringing her hands and questioning him. "Are you sure about this? If it was a cooking class I might hold my own. Slapping paint on squares of stretched canvas is so far out of my comfort zone, I'm going to make a proper fool of myself."

Fen had his leg brace on and locked, which meant he sat in the back seat of Thelma's four-door pickup. "You'll do fine. Pretend you're in the kitchen back home and Bailey comes to you and says she wants to give you a birthday present. She hands you six sketches to choose from. You inspect them and select the one you like best."

"But these kids aren't Bailey. She'd know ahead of time what I like and don't like. Of course that wouldn't stop us going three or four rounds disagreeing with one another. That gal can hold her own when it comes to having an opinion. I need to know someone for a while before I can have a decent word fight with them."

"You're over-thinking this."

She snapped back, "You keep saying that but these are high school kids. I don't want to hurt their feelings."

"They're tougher than you think; and if they're not, they need to learn that not everyone will like what they draw and paint. For commissions it's about pleasing the customer." He paused and decreased his rate of speech. "Besides, you brought them cookies. Everyone understands cookies, especially when they're as good as yours."

"Horsefeathers! When you turn on the compliments, I know there's a pit for me to fall in. This will not end well. I can tell because my left eye is twitching. That's always a sure sign."

Once inside Fen called the class to order and asked if they understood their assignment. One at a time, they'd bring their sketches and the preliminary work they'd done on their painting. He then threw them a bit of a curveball. If they wanted to choose a different landscape from the one they originally chose, they could do so. However, the cutoff for committing to a sketch that would become a final painting would be the next morning at nine o'clock. He wanted to see how committed they were to their original choice.

One at a time, the students filed into a small room where Fen sat with his leg propped on a chair. Thelma looked like a squirrel caught in the open between two trees, not knowing which way to run. She pulled herself together, complimented the first three students on the quality of their sketches, and made her selection. He watched as doubt pulled down the smiles from two students' faces when Thelma's choice didn't match the ones they'd selected.

Fen had his speeches prepared for both possibilities. To those whose selection matched Thelma's, he said, "Thelma chose the same sketch you did. That doesn't mean much. All you have is one person's opinion and your own. The judges may look for something completely different. Also, your finished painting must meet the highest standards if you hope to win."

The other students, when Thelma's selection didn't match their own, got a variation of the one-person's-opinion speech with a caution for them to remember the judges would be the final votes that counted.

Things were going fine until P.B. handed Thelma only two sketches. "Honey child, where's the other four?"

"That's all I did," said the girl dressed for a funeral with a face of white powder and eyeliner as thick and black as a chimney-sweep's brush.

Fen took over. "That's a bold decision to submit only two."

She slowly turned her head and focused on him. "I'm a bold artist. I take risks. That's the way I live and the way I paint. Am I disqualified from the competition?"

"No. Do you want Thelma to tell you which sketch she likes the best?"

"It won't change what I'm going to paint."

All the while, Thelma had been staring at the two sketches. "This is like comparing an apple pie and a chocolate cake. Up to now I've had one stand out and sort of tell me to pick it. Both of these are talking to me, and they're talking loud."

A quirk of a smile flickered across P.B.'s top lip, then was gone.

Fen rubbed his chin. "P.B., you've done the impossible—stumped Thelma. Tell me in the morning if it's going to be a river scene or the one of the lake."

"Both." P.B. shifted her dark eyes back to Thelma. "Do I still get cookies?"

Thelma handed her two plastic bags. "Honey, I'm one of the most opinionated people you'll ever meet. You get double."

He asked, "Don't you have a canvas to show me? An outline?"

She swung her short, black hair from side to side. "I didn't know what I was going to paint until now. I'll work on it tonight and bring it in the morning."

"By the way," said Fen. "I heard one student and her mother played a dirty trick on you this morning."

With a flip of her wrist, P.B. dismissed the statement. "You needn't worry about that, especially with your leg the way it is. The universe has a way of settling scores."

"I don't mind it when the universe evens things up; it's when people help it along that things get out of hand. I hope you're not planning to get even."

"All they did was try to embarrass me. Good luck with that. Don't worry. I won't inflict any physical harm or destroy any property."

"Glad to hear it. I look forward to seeing your canvas in the morning."

The door closed and Thelma looked at him with wide eyes. "I like that gal. She's got more brass than an army bugle band. Don't get me wrong. If she were mine I'd take soap and a warm washcloth to her face and scrub it until the pretty underneath shone through."

Next up was Holly. She handed her sketches to Thelma and chewed a fingernail. Thelma took her time examining the six sketches.

"Holly, you look distracted," said Fen.

She brought her finger down from her mouth. "Sorry. Mom's rented a cabin and is staying close to town until the competition is over."

"Do you feel more pressure when she's around?"

She shrugged. "Sometimes, but not usually. She's not real pushy, but I can tell she wants me to beat Candice at least once before I go to college."

"Will you study art?"

She shook her head. "I'll take some classes as electives and I might talk Grandpa Gilmore into allowing me to get a minor in art, but they set my future in stone. I'm to be a banker."

Fen scratched his ear. "You don't sound excited about it."

"Mom understands. She'd never admit it, but she'd like to bust free, too."

"But?"

Holly shrugged. "You'd have to meet my grandpa to understand."

"Perhaps I will. Is he coming to the competition?"

She tilted her head. "I'm surprised you haven't met him yet. His banks are the primary sponsors of this competition and he chose you to guide us students these two weeks."

"That's interesting," said Fen, as he looked at a spot on the wall. He brought his gaze back to Holly. "Did he also pick the judges?"

Holly looked at the floor. "There's a committee that picks the judges. I don't think grandpa did anything to cheat, but he's keeping a close eye on things to make sure no one else does. He wants me to win fair and square, and knows why I haven't in the past."

Thelma looked at him to see if he wanted to continue his questions. He gave a shake of his head, so she said, "These are all first-rate, but this sketch of the park is definitely my choice."

"That's the one I chose, too. It's not my favorite, but I think it has the most commercial potential."

Fen gave her a big smile. "You and I think alike. Paint what you love, but bend to the desires of the customer when you need to. Show me what you've done so far on your canvas."

Students came and went. "How many more?" asked Thelma. "I'm running low on cookies."

Fen ran a finger down a typed page. Each name had a

check beside it but one. "Last customer, and we saved the best for last. Tell Candice she can come in."

It didn't surprise Fen when Jewell walked in with all the confidence of royalty, followed by her daughter.

Neither he nor Thelma got a word in before Jewell said, "So sorry to barge in without an invitation. I thought I'd take Candice to supper tonight and didn't realize she allowed the other students to go before her. She's so unselfish. Anyway, now that I'm here, I hope you don't mind if I sit in on this unique teaching experience. Candice has never had to submit her sketches for approval."

Fen faked a smile. "I'm afraid there's been some sort of miscommunication. She isn't submitting the sketches for approval or disapproval."

"Then what's the purpose of this exercise?"

"To teach the students a valuable lesson about being an artist." He nodded to Thelma, who stretched her hand toward Candice. "Let me look at them, sugar, and I'll tell you which one I'd like to see made into a nice painting."

Candice handed over the sketches. Jewell took in a gasping breath. "I must protest, Mr. Maguire. I don't know this woman. What are her qualifications?"

"You don't know her because she's my cook and housekeeper," said Fen with a wide smile. He offered no further explanation.

Thelma moved to a sketch of the river and placed it on top of the others. "All six are very good, but this one caught my attention the most."

Candice looked at her mother and shook her head.

"This is ridiculous," said Jewell with arms crossed. "It's obvious this woman knows nothing about symmetry or style."

Fen shrugged. "The only thing she knows is what she likes.

It's not a critique, only one person's opinion. Many of the students have never sold their works in a public setting—"

She cut him off. "Of course not. People who appreciate her talent buy Candice's works. Not the general public."

Fen continued by paraphrasing and completing his interrupted sentence. "Many students have never sold a painting in a public setting. That means they've had none of their works rejected. Even professional critics can't agree on what's good and what's great."

"Candice is a superior artist, and that's the end of this conversation."

"No, it's not. Certain people judged some of Michelangelo's works to be substandard. It's part of being an artist."

"What do they know?"

"People know what they like and what they don't like."

Crimson had crept up Jewell's neck, which told him she had more to say.

"I'll have you know that Candice has sold dozens of paintings and each person raved about them."

"How many people commissioned them?"

"What difference does that make? Can't you understand? She's the best."

Fen didn't back down. "You didn't answer my question."

"That's none of your business."

"Fair enough, but if anyone wants to become an artist, they will face rejection sooner or later. It happens to everyone."

Candice's chin quivered as she asked, "Mom, did you talk all those people into buying my paintings?"

Jewell's eyes turned to molten coals peering through slits as she looked at Fen.

It seemed she was too mad to speak, so Fen said, "Candice, your mom's right. You're a talented artist who could become even better, much better, possibly even great, someday."

"Enough!" shouted Jewell. "Candice, come with me. I've heard enough from this hayseed philosopher. You're destined for greatness and I'll let nothing stand in your way."

Candice shook her head while looking down. "You go on to supper, Mom. I'm staying here to work on my painting. I want to win, but I don't want you doing whatever it is you've done in the past to make it happen. This time I want to succeed or fail on my own."

"What nonsense." Jewell kept her gaze on Fen as her words came out sounding like someone wrote them for a British play set in a stately manor house. "This comes from having you associate with the wrong type of people. I should have known better than to enter you in this backwater competition."

She shifted her gaze to her daughter. "You must believe me, dear, you'll forget this clap trap from these rubes about failure after you take first place again. There's nothing better than a victory to put you to rights. Come along. We'll have a nice supper and you'll feel better."

"Not tonight, Mom. I feel a migraine coming on."

Jewell shot an accusatory look at both Fen and Thelma. "I hold both of you responsible. Expect consequences." She turned back to Candice. "Take your medicine and get a good night's sleep, dear. You'll feel much better in the morning. I'll meet you for yoga."

Jewell stormed out the door leaving a waft of expensive perfume behind her. Candice collected her sketches and followed in her mother's wake. Thelma stood, shut the door, and turned to Fen. "I'm not sure what a rube is but I know a witch when I see one. That woman must get around on a broom."

Fen didn't comment other than to say, "It will be interesting to see how she plans to make sure Candice wins. Holly's grandfather is keeping a close eye on things to make sure the contest is fair and square."

Thelma stood. "Is playing games with other people's lives the only thing rich people have to do?"

Fen shrugged. If he said anything else, he'd have to listen to one of Thelma's rants. Most likely he would anyway. The trip home proved him right, as did sitting through supper with her. As soon as he could, he took a pain pill and went to bed.

The effects of the pill were pulling his eyelids down when his phone rang. He propped an extra pillow behind his head after seeing Lou's name. A groggy salutation came forth.

"Are you in bed already? It's not even seven-thirty."

"I took a pain pill. Make it quick unless you want to listen to me snore."

"It's not much, but I thought you might like to know about Jewell's exes Jeremy and Cliff. They're both on their way to jail after they make a stop by the hospital. Another fight in the bar. This time it was like something from an old western movie with chairs broken and tables turned over. They'll both need stitches."

"What set them off this time?"

"It seems Jewell made dates with both of them. Drinks at the hotel bar, followed by dinner at that Mexican restaurant we were supposed to go to."

"Hold on. My mind is getting fuzzy. Are you saying she planned to go out with both exes at the same time?"

"You got it. She sat at a table and watched them go at each other."

"I'm not surprised she'd do something like that. She and I had a bit of a spat this afternoon."

"Uh-huh. Can you tell me about it?"

"Not without slurring my words. Chalk it up to different philosophies related to sales and marketing."

"I'll give you a pass tonight, but you're giving me the full story tomorrow. After the fight I went to her room. She wasn't there. Do you know if she had other plans for the evening?"

"All I know is Jewell left campus without Candice this afternoon. You might try calling Bailey to see if Candice changed her mind. Jewell wanted to have a mother-daughter dinner."

"I called her. Candice is on campus but wasn't in the mood to discuss her mother."

It was in the wee hours of the morning when he awoke and realized the phone had slipped from his hand while he was talking to Lou. No more pain pills unless he re-injured his knee.

Chapter Twelve

D ays later, Fen was in his chair enjoying a pre-dawn cup of coffee when an insistent knock sounded on the door. His mind raced back to the bangs on his door when a Kerrville police officer informed him of Rose Cunningham's murder. He gripped the arms of the recliner and pushed up.

Thelma had left the day before, after he abandoned the crutches and knee brace and assured her he'd call if his knee popped out of place again. She'd stayed six nights and five days.

Not wanting to repeat sharing a condo with his housekeeper and cook, he gingerly stood and tested his knee before taking tentative steps toward the sound of more knocks. He opened the door and his heart seemed to sink a couple of inches within his chest. Before him stood Officer Brent Craven with bad news painted across his unsmiling face.

Fen asked, "Is it Jewell?"

The officer nodded.

"Same place?"

"On this side of the dam."

Fen told Officer Craven he needed to use the restroom and grab his wallet before he could go.

"Make it quick. The chief's mad as a shaved porcupine."

Fen closed his bedroom door, pulled out his phone, and placed a call to Lou as he went into the bathroom. He then closed that door behind him for extra privacy. It took six rings before she answered. He didn't give her a chance to chastise him for the early call. "You can stop looking for Jewell. Get dressed and go to the park where they do sunrise yoga. They found her body in the Guadalupe." He disconnected the call, not giving her a chance to barrage him with questions he didn't have the answers to.

The first part of the ride to the park was a grim replay of the trip when they found Rose Cunningham's body. The only difference was this light-and-siren trip took place earlier in the day. The first pinkish streaks of light didn't crest the hills to the east until after they arrived. They turned right on Highway 16 and crossed the bridge, went a short distance, and pulled into the parking lot. Most of the first responders had pulled their vehicles to within a stone's throw of the smooth water, creating a visual barrier to what was taking place.

Officer Craven came to a stop on grass where picnics usually took place. The chief of police gave the young officer a nod of approval and said, "Get with Ramos and put up crime-scene tape. Make a perimeter of fifty yards."

With the order given, Ben Strange shifted his gaze to Fen. "We thought her disappearing again was another publicity stunt. I was waiting seventy-two hours from the first report of her going missing. Now my neck is in a noose if I don't get this solved in a big hurry."

"That's not all," said Fen. "Your case against Ray-Ray is looking mighty weak."

Ben pulled a hand down his face. "I thought of that on my

way here. All I can prove is that he took credit cards from a purse he found in the river. There's no DNA evidence that shows he touched anything but her purse." He looked past the lake to the city on the far bank. "I know how these things work. It won't be long before someone uses the term *serial killer* and tourism falls off. You can bet your last dollar it won't be the mayor or DA receiving the blame."

Fen put his hand on the chief's shoulder. "The best thing to do is discover who killed both women and get that person or persons behind bars. I'll be glad to help."

"You don't know how glad I am to hear you say that." His gaze shifted to Fen. "The owner of a local donut shop spotted something in the water on his way to work this morning. He mentioned it to an officer on the night shift who was in for his morning coffee. He stopped on the bridge and used his car's spotlight. Fire and Rescue launched a boat within twenty minutes of receiving the call. They believe she's been in the water for quite a while."

"Hours or days?"

"At least two days. They couldn't leave her there or she might go over the spillway. Everyone that touched the body had on gloves so hopefully they didn't contaminate any evidence. When I saw who it was I put a call in for a state forensics team to get here as soon as they could."

Fen cast his gaze toward the body of water. "The problem with a death in a river is finding the original crime scene. That's where the forensics crew will want to focus their efforts. You'll need to send your men upstream to look for any sign of a struggle or physical evidence."

"I have every person I can spare on their way to help. The sheriff is sending all the help he can."

"I assume you've looked at the body?"

Ben nodded. "I'd appreciate it if you'd look at her and tell me what you think."

Fen nodded and moved with Ben to the Zodiac boat with its bow pulled onto dry land. First responders parted as they approached. In the bottom of the inflatable craft lay a lifeless body, face up, with eyes closed.

With a nod of his head Fen whispered, "It's Jewell, all right." He pointed. "I recognize the small tattoo on the inside of her ankle. It's her daughter's name." He scanned the clothes and jewelry. "If this is a robbery gone bad, whoever killed her left behind a small fortune in gold and diamonds. I wouldn't rule it out, but it seems unlikely."

"What about the bruising on her neck?" asked Ben.

Fen raised his head. "Who has a flashlight?"

Two officers pulled small but powerful flashlights from their utility belts and took up stations on either side, one standing ankle deep in water.

"Put the light on her neck." He leaned over to get a better look and spoke as he straightened. "The discoloration isn't what you'd expect in a strangulation. If someone's hands did it, you'd see bruising around the entire neck, cutting off blood and air. From what I can see, the discoloration doesn't extend to the back of the neck."

Ben's eyebrows raised. "What does that mean?"

Fen raised his shoulders and let them drop. "You'll know more when you get the results from the autopsy, but it looks to me like someone took something like a pipe or round bar and pushed down hard on the front of her throat."

Ben took a step back. "Let's take a walk."

The chief's idea of a walk was to go to his SUV and have a conversation away from everyone else. After the doors closed, the chief pivoted in his seat to face him. "Let's review what we have so far. About a week ago, someone killed Rose Cunningham. We arrested Ray-Ray, but now with Jewell dead I'm not so sure. Do you believe she was mistaken for Jewell?"

"I can't say for sure, but it's somewhere between possible and probable, leaning toward the latter."

Ben gave his head a nod. "And I screwed up by taking the easy way out once I had a suspect in custody." He cast his gaze toward the lake. "I knew I shouldn't have stopped digging."

He wanted to tell Ben not to beat himself up but didn't. The chief of police was right. Pressure from the mayor and DA wasn't a good enough excuse to not investigate. Instead of commiserating he said, "I work with an investigative reporter. She'll be here any minute. You may have stopped digging, but she didn't."

Ben's voice came out with renewed hope. "Please tell me she has something to help me crack that case."

"She'll turn over everything she's done. So far there's no link between Rose and Jewell. Absolutely nothing."

Ben's hope seemed to melt. "What good does that do me?"

"Ben, stop worrying and start thinking. You're a smart guy. If there's no link between the two women except their looks, that tells you a lot. I believe we're looking at three possibilities. One is that Rose's death was a random act of violence. The second is, we're looking for a serial killer who targets beautiful women with long black hair."

"That's my worst nightmare."

"Mine, too. If that's the case, there'll be a state, federal, and local task force set up. All it will take is one more woman in the river who looks similar to Jewell and Rose."

"What's the third possibility?"

"Jewell was the target but the killer mistook Rose Cunningham for her." He took a breath. "Going on that assumption, what can we extrapolate?"

He waited for Ben to come up with an answer. After half a

minute of silence Fen said, "Someone hated Jewell enough to press through with killing her, even after they'd killed an innocent woman. It's time to line up suspects who had something against Jewell, and there are plenty to choose from. I can name five or six off the top of my head that are here in town. Always start with family and work your way out."

"The only family Jewell is close to is her daughter. You don't think..."

His words trailed off and Fen said, "I'll talk to Candice as well as any students that had something against Jewell or Candice. There's one parent of a student I'll also need to talk to."

"What about me?" asked the chief.

"I'm not sure if they're still in town, but I understand your department had dealings with two ex-husbands this week."

"That's right. They've been banging on my desk for three days demanding I find her. They were like two bucks chasing the same doe. What if the doe chose one over the other? That could motivate one of them to kill Jewell."

"We still can't rule out her death as being random. Everything is still on the table."

Bright sunshine shone through the trees. The city was coming to life. Fen looked toward the parking lot. "I need to head Lou off before she peppers you with questions. I'm surprised the mayor isn't here yet."

Ben slapped his forehead. "I haven't called him yet. My goose is halfway cooked and it's not even eight o'clock yet."

Fen made sure his foot didn't slip when he stepped out of the SUV. He passed the justice of the peace who ignored him, which was fine. It wasn't a morning for pleasantries.

Heading his way was Bailey, wearing the standard yoga uniform, leggings and a snug T-shirt. She waited for him to speak. "Lou should be here any minute. I'll explain to both of you at the same time."

Right on cue, Lou came toward them at a trot. "Can I get close enough to get photos and video?"

"It'll have to be from fifty yards away, but that will give me a chance to tell you what's going on."

They moved to a spot that gave them the most unobstructed view and Lou went to work alternating between taking short videos and photos. When she had enough to satisfy television and newspaper editors, she turned to him. "Make it snappy. I'll need to get this out ASAP."

Fen started with the owner of the donut shop spotting something in the lake and ended with his talk with Chief Strange. "I told him you'd turn over all the research you did on Rose Cunningham. He expects it today. Add what you've done on Jewell. The chief's detectives don't impress me as being the sharpest knives in the drawer."

She looked away and huffed. "All those years I spent guarding my sources. I'm still not used to doing the cop's job for them."

Bailey broke in. "Brent told me Roy had to cancel yoga classes today."

Fen said, "Go back to the university and don't repeat anything I said. Play like you don't know what's going on."

She nodded. "I doubt anyone will ask me. Several of the girls are in the parking lot; they'll be the ones spilling the story. I came with Holly this morning. She's pumping Roy for information."

Fen took his turn again. "I'm going to the university. The cops will notify Candice this morning and I'll tell them I'll look after her until I hear otherwise. I want you to keep an eye on Holly and P.B. They both had something against Jewell. Let me know tonight how they reacted to the news of her death."

"What if I invite them to bring some of their works to sell at the booth I set up tomorrow? I could monitor them there, too."

"Good idea. We'll all meet tonight at the condo."

Lou shook her head. "I'd love to be a fly on the wall when Chief Strange interviews the two ex-husbands."

"That's a good idea. Try to get to them before the chief or his detectives."

Lou puffed out her cheeks. "I've watched the paint dry in my hotel room for three days, and now I have ten things to do and time for only five. First thing first: video to the television stations. Next, I'll get interviews with Chief Strange and the mayor and fire chief. After that, I'll go to the donut shop." She turned toward the parking lot. "There's the mayor coming as fast as his stubby legs can carry him. Call or text if either of you hear anything new."

Fen and Bailey watched as Lou intercepted the mayor and walked with him toward the lake. Bailey was the first to speak. "She can go from a dead stop to a hundred miles an hour faster than anyone I've ever seen."

"She's had years of practice," said Fen with a touch of admiration in his voice. The two walked to the parking lot at a pace reflecting caution for his healing knee. As they approached his truck, he noticed an attractive woman speaking with Holly. He asked, "Didn't I hear that Holly's mother was coming to town? Is that her?"

Bailey shrugged. "She's rented a cabin nearby, right on the river. Holly said she's staying until the competition is over, but that woman looks too young to have a daughter that's seventeen."

"Not necessarily. It all depends on how old Holly's mom was when she got pregnant." He craned his head toward Bailey. "Let's go talk to them. I want to see their reaction to the news of Jewell's death."

Chapter Thirteen

Holly's brow wrinkled into a question as Fen and Bailey approached, but it was the woman with her who spoke first. "Do you know what's going on?"

Fen gave his head a nod. "I'm afraid I do." He extended a hand. "I'm Fen Maguire and this is Bailey Madison."

Holly broke in, "Mom, Mr. Maguire is our instructor. Bailey is an artist in her own right who helps us in the dorm." She tilted her head toward her mother. "This is my mother, Cindi Gilmore."

From Lou's research, he knew Cindi wasn't married, and that she'd never been married. He wondered about the birth father. It was one of those blank spots in Lou's research that would need filling in. He extended a hand. "Your daughter is exceptionally talented."

She dipped her chin. "Thank you."

While shaking hands he took in details about the petite, blond woman. The first thought that came to his mind was that she looked like a former high school cheerleader, except for the worry lines radiating out from Caribbean-blue eyes.

She was a handsome woman, in a cute sort of way, but her eyes held sadness. He would have missed it if he hadn't studied eyes so much while trying to capture Sally's in her portrait.

It was time to focus on mother and daughter and their reactions to the news of Jewell's untimely demise. "There's been a death."

Holly spoke up. "That's what Roy said."

"Who's Roy?" asked Cindi.

Holly and Bailey answered at the same time. "Our yoga instructor."

They looked at each other and smiled. "Sorry," said Bailey. "Fen tells me my mouth works better than my ears."

Fen fixed his gaze on Cindi. "I believe you know the victim. It's Jewell Key."

A sharp intake of air and wide-open eyes marked Cindi's response. Holly shook her head in disbelief and said, "That's horrible. Are you sure it's Candice's mom? Does she know?"

"I don't see Candice's car. She didn't come to yoga today?" asked Fen.

Bailey and Holly looked at each other and shook their heads. "We haven't seen her," said Holly.

He took out his phone and placed a call to Chief Strange.

"Make it quick, Fen."

"Candice didn't come to the yoga class this morning. It's likely she's still at the university. Do you want me to notify her or would you rather send an officer?"

The response was immediate. "Every person I can scrounge up is looking for the original crime scene. You'd do me a big favor if you told her. Do you know who the next of kin is?"

"After her daughter it's ex-husband number one, according to Lou Cooper."

"Thanks. I'll ask her."

"Expect her to make a deal. It will probably cost you a quick interview."

"We want to get ahead of the story so that shouldn't be a problem."

The call ended without the normal salutations so he pocketed the phone and turned to Cindi. "Could you come to the university?"

"Right now?"

He nodded. "They cook a decent breakfast and it's a good thing to keep your blood sugar up after hearing disturbing news."

Bailey looked at Holly. "That goes for you, too."

Mother and daughter looked at each other and nodded.

"Good," he said, looking at Cindi. "I'll give you a tour of the art studio after breakfast."

The four went to their vehicles and drove to campus. As he drove Fen considered the best way to glean information from Cindi without coming right out and asking her if she killed Jewell. She didn't fit the profile, but he'd learned a long time ago that people will surprise you. As he turned into the campus, another thought came to his mind. What about Cindi's father? He knew Jewell had done plenty of underhanded things to ensure his granddaughter came in second place to Candice. His mind took off like a spinning dust devil. Jewell's murder was twisting into a case with too many suspects.

Fen arrived in the parking lot and saw Bailey walking toward him. "Do you want me to get Holly away from her mom while you question her?"

"I don't want it to be that obvious. Let's eat together and then you do something that will leave me alone with her mom."

"Like what?"

His top lip quirked. "You're the detective-in-training. Impress me with your creativity."

She took up the challenge. "All right, I will."

The two of them walked across the parking lot to where Holly and her mom were waiting for them. Fen kept the conversation light, talking about his knee and how much he was looking forward to seeing the progress the students made while he was out recuperating. The foursome went through the food line then found a table away from other students.

As they settled at the table, Fen looked at Cindi. "I hope you'll join me in the studio and give me your opinion on the works in progress."

She spoke in a soft voice. "I'd love to see the works, but talent for painting skipped me. Holly got a double-dose."

"What about Holly's father? Is he an artist?"

Cindi dipped her head as Holly answered for her. "My father died before I was born."

"I'm so sorry. I didn't know."

Holly shrugged. "Grandpa Gilmore did double duty. He's like a cuddly drill sergeant."

Fen chuckled. "That would be a challenge to paint. I understand his banks are sponsoring the contest. I look forward to meeting him."

"He's coming back to town today." Holly looked at her mother. "Mom, do you know when?"

"Sometime this morning. Knowing him, it will be early."

Fen asked, "Do you think he'd have time to come here? I'd love to meet him."

Cindi nodded. "He said something about making a surprise visit to the class. He likes to do things like that with his banks. Says it keeps people on their toes."

"He sounds like a wise business owner."

Holly nodded with vigor. "He is, and stubborn as they come. That's how he got his nickname of Stony."

Fen looked to Cindi. His raised eyebrows asked her to

confirm or deny her father's personality trait. She replied, "My grandfather called him Stony, and it stuck. I'm afraid Holly's right. He has definite opinions. He might not always express them, but they're just under the surface."

Fen wondered *if stubborn and definite opinions* meant he had a mean streak running through him. Perhaps it was one wide enough to do away with a woman who'd been a thorn in his side ever since Jewell made it her business to ensure Candice won every competition she took part in. He'd need to check to see when Stony Gilmore was last in town.

While he pondered, Cindi's phone rang. She dug it out of her purse and said, "Excuse me. It's my father."

After a minute or two, she thrust the phone toward Fen. "He wants to talk to you."

Fen took the phone from Cindi. "Hello, Mr. Gilmore."

"Maguire, is it true? Is Jewell dead?"

"Yes, sir. I helped identify her."

"Was it an accident?"

Fen considered giving him the standard non-committal answer but decided against it. This was a man who could handle the unvarnished truth. "It has all the markings of a homicide."

"Are you helping the police?"

"They've asked me to consult on this death and Rose Cunningham's."

"I'm three minutes away. We need to talk. Tell Cindi to meet me in the parking lot."

Fen handed the silent phone back to Cindi. "He'll be here in three minutes. He wants you to meet him in the parking lot."

Bailey stood and looked at Holly. "That's our cue to leave."

Holly put her hands on the table and pushed her chair back. "You don't need to tell me twice. I've heard that tone of voice from my grandpa before. Let's hide in the art studio."

Fen thought about having another cup of coffee while he waited alone in the dining room. He decided against it and watched the last student rise to leave. P.B. stopped by his table, wearing all-black as usual. "I hear they found Candice's mother in the river this morning."

Fen nodded. "Bad news has wings. How did you find out?"

"My dad called me."

"Your dad?"

"Judge Brown. The local justice of the peace. He told me you're helping with the investigation."

Fen knew better than to deny it with this bright, well-informed student. "Any ideas of who might have killed her?"

She shrugged. "If you're talking about students, Holly had the most reasons to do it, but she wasn't the only one who'd been screwed-over by Candice's mom."

"Including you?"

"Including me, and before you ask, I don't have an alibi for three nights ago. I break into the art studio at night and paint by myself."

Fen tilted his head. "You sleep during the day and paint at night?"

She nodded. "I'm going to bed now."

He rubbed his chin. "Whatever works for you is fine with me. I'll leave the studio unlocked for you."

"No need. Bailey's not the only one who knows how to pick a lock."

"Did she tell you that?"

"She didn't need to. We have more in common than you think."

"One thing," said Fen. "Candice hasn't been told yet about her mother."

"She won't hear it from me. I'm going to the dorm."

Through the door came Cindi and a man with a shock of

thick, gray hair. P.B. made a wide loop around them on her way out.

Fen stood and offered a hand to shake. He received a stronger-than-necessary grip.

"Stony Gilmore," said the man as his grey eyes locked on him. "What can you tell me about Jewell Key's death?"

Fen motioned with a hand for Mr. Gilmore and Cindi to have a seat. "Cindi's not staying. Where's Holly?"

"All the students are in the art studio or on their way there. The chief of police asked me to tell Candice about her mother so this will need to be quick."

"Then get to it."

He took a breath. "We won't know the day or approximate time of death until after the autopsy, but from the condition of the body, I'd say Jewell has been in the river for three days. That coincides with when her two ex-husbands reported her missing. The police didn't make a big deal of it because—"

Stony interrupted. "Because they thought it was another publicity stunt."

Fen nodded.

"What makes you sure it's a homicide and not an accident?"

"Excessive bruising on her neck."

"They strangled her?"

"I didn't say that."

Stony pursed his lips in a way that showed he didn't like the answer but he moved on. "Who found the body?"

"A Kerrville police officer after receiving a tip of something floating in the river."

"Who told the police?"

"The owner of a donut shop."

The older man nodded.

Fen stood. "I've put off telling Candice long enough. In

fact, I'll need to tell all the students to expect the police to question them unless they find hard evidence today that results in someone else's arrest."

"Does that include Holly?"

Fen nodded. "Think of it as throwing a rock in a pond on a calm day. The circles radiate out. The investigation will start with family, then close friends. Next will be anyone with something against Jewell."

"That would include Holly and Cindi." He narrowed his eyes. "I don't like it."

"I don't blame you." Fen paused. "You can also add your name to the list."

He responded with a glare.

Fen gave him an alternative. "There's a way to avoid a formal interview by the police."

"What's that?"

"I can interview each of you today. I'll ask the same questions they would."

"Can I have my attorney present?"

"I won't stop you from it, but the cops may think you're trying to hide something."

He looked away but only for a few seconds. "Can I sit in while you talk to Holly and Cindi?"

It contradicted what Fen knew to be proper interview techniques, but something in his gut told him to make an exception to the rules... at least a partial exception. "I'm going to interview them separately after I finish your questioning. I'll allow you to sit in as long as you let your daughter and granddaughter answer my questions without you interfering or coaching them."

"I'll agree as long as you don't trick them or bully them. I'm not worried about me."

Fen nodded. "I'll ask straight questions and expect straight answers."

"That sounds fair enough." He leaned forward. "Cross my girls on this and I'll come after you with everything I have."

"I'd do the same if it were my daughter and granddaughter."

Fen's next stop would be the low point of his day—telling Candice her mother was dead.

Chapter Fourteen

Instead of going into the art studio, Fen sent Bailey to fetch Candice and bring her to the office the university had assigned him to use. It technically qualified as an office because it had a desk, a well-used executive chair, and two chairs that looked to be discarded from an army surplus store. Otherwise, it had the dimensions of a small storage closet and no windows. It was his first time to put the key in the lock and turn the handle.

A few minutes later, Bailey opened the door and stood back as Candice strode confidently into the room. With a defiant look, the girl stood behind a chair, using it as a barrier. He narrowed the distance by perching on the front edge of the desk. The door closed before he could say anything. Bailey had made her escape.

"Who told on me?" demanded Candice.

He hoped he succeeded in not looking surprised as he considered asking her what mischief she'd been up to. Whatever it was, it didn't rise to the level of what he had to say to her. "Bailey didn't bring you here because of what you may or may not have done. I have bad news, and it would be best if you sat down."

She raised her chin an inch. "I'll stand."

"Suit yourself. I'm glad you didn't go to the early morning yoga class today."

She rolled her eyes. "I only went to check it out and then Mom insisted I go with her. I haven't been back since she stood me up three days ago."

"She's no longer missing."

Instead of allowing him to finish telling her about her mother, she answered with a comment of her own. "Thanks for telling me." She rolled her eyes. "Another of the mind games she plays when I'm in a competition. She's usually more creative."

"Like I said, she's not missing anymore." He hated this next part. "There's no easy way for me to say what I have to, so get a good grip on the back of the chair. Your mother's body was found this morning."

The words seemed to bounce off her and land on the floor. "Good one, Mr. Maguire. Can I go now? Mom will be furious that I haven't made more progress on my painting."

Fen stood. "This morning before daylight, a Kerrville police officer banged on my door. I followed his patrol car to the river that runs by the park you're painting. First responders pulled your mother's body out of the water before first light. She'd been there a long time. I saw her."

She shook her head. "I don't believe you, and you can get into a lot of trouble for making up such a horrible story. Mom's always working an angle. If it's not to help me win, it's finding the next rich man or some boy-toy to play with."

"If you don't believe me, I can call the police and have an officer come and tell you the same thing. The story will be on the news within the hour if they haven't already broadcast it. If you'd gone to yoga this morning, you'd have seen it all for your-self." Fen paused. "The chief of police asked me to tell you instead of sending someone you don't know."

Candice's chin quivered as she worked her way around the chair and sat down. She whispered, "You're not lying. I can tell." She looked up through eyes that pooled with tears. "She must have fallen in the river. I hear it's pretty deep in spots and she's a lousy swimmer."

Fen noticed she used the present tense to describe her mother. It was common for people to do so until reality set in. All part of coming to terms with death. She wasn't coming unglued so he gave her the next bit of news. "There's evidence to suggest her death wasn't an accident."

Candice leaned forward, covered her face with her hands, and allowed whatever wall that was holding back her tears to crumble. It lasted about thirty seconds, and then she raised her head and wiped her face with the palms of her hands. "I'm not surprised. The games with her ex-husbands finally caught up with her."

Fen allowed her to talk without interruption. She stared at him. "You're a former state cop and sheriff. You want to know who I think did this to her?" Her voice changed from unbelief to anger. "Take your pick. There's five exes and ten times as many jilted lovers to choose from."

"Which ones stand out to you?"

"Start with the ones who were in town when she went missing. That would be the man who wants me to call him daddy, Jeremy Key."

"He's not your father?"

"Mom says he could be, but I have my doubts. If it's not him, try Cliff Rouse, husband number two. Mom was toying with them, giving them false hope that they could win her back.

It was all part of her plan to see how much she could get out of an ex-husband the second time around."

"She planned on marrying one of them again?"

Candice crossed her legs and leaned back. "Not just one. She was going after all five."

Fen held up his hands. "Let's get back to your mom's death. Is Jeremy Key your next of kin?"

She shrugged. "I'm not sure. You'll have to ask Mom's attorney. Her name is Sylvia Zambrano and her office is in San Antonio."

"I'll call her."

Candice uncrossed her legs. "You can if you want to, but I'm calling her too. None of Mom's husbands were around long enough for me to give a flying fig about them." Her speech increased in rate and intensity. "That includes my biological father, whoever that might be." She paused. "I'll be eighteen the first week of August. I actually graduated last month, but Mom lied on my admission application that my diploma wouldn't be awarded until the end of July. I'm going to tell Ms. Zambrano to do whatever it takes to keep any of mom's exes away from me until I'm fully emancipated."

The grieving child had morphed into a calculating young woman in front of his eyes. Was it possible her mother had trained her too well? He'd think about that later. It was time to tie up a couple of loose ends.

"The person running the contest is here today. I'll ask him to arrange for a grief counselor to stop by and see you."

"That's a waste of time, but I don't want to offend Stony Gilmore. It's going to be hard enough winning against Holly. This time she has the deck stacked in her favor." She shrugged. "Oh well. She may get a trophy, but I'll inherit Mom's millions."

Fen noted that Candice had switched to future tense. He asked, "Are you planning on staying here and competing?"

"Are you going to kick me out because Mom lied on my application?"

"I'm not even going to kick you out for getting drunk last night."

Her eyes darted back and forth as if she was looking for a lie to tell. She then chuckled. "How'd you know?"

"You missed yoga. The smell a person's body secretes the morning after a wild night of drinking has a distinctive odor. Warm, muggy weather and the brisk walk from the dorm made your armpits sweat enough to discolor your blouse. The news of your mom's death was enough to make tiny beads of perspiration form on your forehead."

She stood. "You're smart for an ex-cop turned artist."

"That remains to be seen. I may need to talk to you again."

"We might be able to come to an agreement on that. I'll need all the help I can get if I'm to win this competition."

"That's not what I meant and you know it."

"Sylvia Zambrano may have something to say about me talking to you without an attorney present."

He'd likely get no further information from Candice after she spoke with her attorney. Bailey's value as eyes and ears among the contestants went up another notch.

He had one more question for her. "Do you want to paint today?"

She didn't hesitate. "It all depends on whether Ms. Zambrano wants to come here. If she says we can handle everything over the phone, I'll paint. If she says I need to go to San Antonio, I'll go there and come back as soon as I can." Candice stood. "Is that all?"

He nodded. As soon as the door closed he sent two text messages. The first went to Chief Strange.

Candice informed of mother's death.

The second went to Lou and began with the same words, but he added,

Run the story.

He then checked the imaginary box that read, *Notify Candice* and moved on to the next item on his list: *Tell students.*

HE HEARD the rumble of voices before he opened the door to the art studio. All eyes fixed on him as he limped into the room. There was no easy way of doing this but he could at least make it quick. With hands raised for silence he spoke in a loud, clear voice. "The first thing that happens in situations like this is that rumors fly. I know you've already heard things that are true and some that aren't."

He had everyone's attention so he continued. "It's true that the police found another body in the river upstream from the dam. It's also true that the body is that of Candice's mom, Ms. Jewell Key. Finally, the police believe this to be a homicide." He cast a gaze around the room and asked, "Were any of you downtown before dawn today?"

The students looked at each other with their heads shaking.

"Did any of you sleep anywhere last night except in the dorm?"

Again, all heads shook.

"Very good. Now let's address rumors. Don't pretend you know when or how she died. You'll hear all kinds of stories and at this point they're all speculation or outright fiction. You're here to paint and that's what I expect you to do."

A voice came from the back of the room. "Are you helping with the investigation?"

He wanted to minimize his role, so he answered with a question of his own. "Is there something you need to talk to the police about?"

"Me? Heck no."

Fen scanned the room. "By now I think everyone knows my background. The chief of police asked me to break the news to Candice, which I've done. If anyone here has information related to Ms. Key's death, I'll be glad to pass it on. Otherwise, I came here to help all of you become better artists. That's my priority, and it needs to be yours."

Holly asked, "Is Candice staying in the competition?"

Fen paused before he answered. "A better question to ask is, 'How do we treat her if she stays with us?' The answer is, treat her like you always have and not like she has a contagious disease."

P.B. asked, "Will the cops come here to question us?"

"Like I said a minute ago, if you know anything that you think might be useful, come talk to me."

The room fell silent so he ended his talk with, "As some of you already know, the park is an active crime scene and off limits to everyone. Therefore, use your sketches and photos. To make it fair to everyone, we'll work here today."

"Too darn hot in the afternoon anyway," came a voice.

Fen concluded with, "I have some things to do for the next thirty minutes to an hour. After that I'll be here in the studio all day. This gimpy leg of mine doesn't like me to stand very long, so you'll need to come to me."

He turned his head as Stony walked through the door and nodded to him in acknowledgment. Fen raised his voice. "One more thing. We have with us today the man responsible for this year's competition, Mr. Stony Gilmore. Please show him how much you appreciate his generosity."

A round of applause came forth when Stony raised a hand and waved. He even managed a smile. He then followed Fen out the door. Once they were several steps outside the door, Fen said, "I need some fresh air. Are you up for a short walk around campus?"

"My knees are in good shape. It's yours that has me worried."

"I'm supposed to walk on even surfaces and ride a recumbent stationary bicycle. Let's have a slow walk-and-talk."

"Is this when you give me the third degree?"

Fen grinned. "I don't want you to feel like I short-changed you. Where were you this past Monday, Tuesday, and Wednesday?"

Chapter Fifteen

It was as if nature didn't get the memo that it was supposed to be a somber day. Everything was in full bloom, the temperature, even though the humidity was higher than usual, was in the seventies, and squirrels chased each other around the tree trunks. Fen and Stony walked without talking until a bench under a tree caught their eye. "Let's take a load off. I don't want to press my luck."

Stony was the first to speak after they were seated. "I take it you want me to answer that question about where I was earlier this week?"

"Answering my questions will save you from bothering your attorney or having a detective talk to you. It's no secret that Jewell did a lot of underhanded things to make sure Candice won most every contest she entered. It seems she enjoyed goading Cindi and Holly."

Stony stared at something in the distance. "Jewell was an evil, wicked woman. Whoever killed her rid the world of a parasite."

"Those are mighty strong words."

Stony turned to face him. "True words."

Fen came to gather information, not debate, so he moved on. "Tell me about your week."

Stony turned away. "Good deflection. What you really want to know is, do I have an alibi for when Jewell was killed. Am I right?"

He quirked a smile. "Isn't that what I asked?"

This earned a chuckle. "I guess it was. Cindi wanted to spend her vacation in a cabin by the Guadalupe and be close to Holly in case she needed anything. I thought it was a good idea. She found what she was looking for on VRBO and booked it. We worked at the bank Monday until three in the afternoon. Me at the main bank and her in the branch bank she's running. I followed her to the cabin and spent the night. On all the other nights this week, I was at home in San Antonio. I made day trips to some branches in Austin and Round Rock, but returned home each evening. I have a very good surveillance system at my home. If need be, I can provide the police with video proof of where I was every night except Monday night and early Tuesday morning. I was back at our main bank by eight in the morning on Tuesday."

Stony took a breath. "That reminds me, when was Jewell killed?"

"We won't know until the results of the autopsy come back, but I saw her body. It looked to me like she'd been in the water two to three days, but that's a guess."

"Good thing Cindi and Holly can tell you I was at the rental on Monday night."

"Holly? Did she spend the night?"

"She came to supper and left around nine thirty."

It wasn't an air-tight alibi, but if the coroner determined Jewell died after about six o'clock on Tuesday, it would eliminate Stony from the list of suspects. Time to dig deeper. "Who's Holly's father?"

Stony jerked his head around and glared. "None of your business."

Fen didn't expect such a reaction. He wanted to know why he'd touched such a raw nerve, so he backed away from a frontal attack and hit him from the side. "It doesn't matter if you tell me or not, but if you don't the police will haul Cindi in for questioning. They won't be delicate in how they ask her."

"It's none of their business either."

Fen shrugged. "Have it your way, but you're only delaying the inevitable."

Stony seemed to consider his options before allowing the information to seep out. "He was a worthless piece of trash who got Cindi pregnant when she was seventeen. I paid him off and told him to get out of the state."

"What else did you tell him?"

"I warned him that if he ever came back, I would bury him in a deep hole somewhere between here and Mexico. I hired a private investigator to keep track of him for five years. The last I heard he was living in California."

"And his name?"

The response came out sounding like a snake's hiss. "Roger Slade."

The next minute passed in silence. The time seemed to settle Stony's anger. He asked, "Why did you make me bring up such an unpleasant memory?"

"Good question," said Fen. "It's important in a murder investigation to tie up all the loose ends. Roger Slade is a loose end."

"I don't understand."

Fen turned to him. "You're a father who protects your

daughter and granddaughter. Like it or not, Roger Slade is a father, too."

"He's never been a father to Holly and never will be."

"I believe you, but until we find out where he was when Jewell died, he's still a suspect." He quickly added, "Don't let the word suspect throw you. There's a long list of them at this stage of the investigation. Ninety-five percent of the information gathered doesn't mean a thing."

"Am I a suspect?"

"Of course. You, Cindi, and even Holly are suspects because Jewell did things to harm all of you."

Fen kept talking. "You loan large amounts of money to people and I bet you require them to provide you with lots of information."

Stony nodded. "I see what you're getting at. I have to pay attention to the little things or I'll make a big mistake."

"Exactly. If you, Cindi, and Holly had nothing to do with Jewell's death, then nothing bad will show up. Think of an investigation as a request for a loan."

"I don't like it that Cindi and Holly are suspects."

"Believe me," said Fen. "The line of people with a motive for killing Jewell is long. It's also possible that her death was a random killing. It will take time and proof to solve this one."

"Do you still need to talk to Cindi and Holly?"

He nodded. "If I don't, they'll be loose ends."

Stony stood. "Let's get this over with."

Fen took out his phone and sent Bailey a text. Her reply came back as they walked toward the dining room. He told Stoney what the text said. "Cindi will meet us in the dining room. The coffee here isn't great, but it's hot and there's always plenty of it."

Bailey and Cindi were sitting at a table when he and Stony arrived. Fen took a detour and retrieved a cup of coffee. Bailey met him as he filled a white porcelain cup and asked, "Do you need me to stay?"

"Not this time."

Bailey huffed. "I thought you were going to let me help with this investigation. How can I do that if you do all the work?"

Fen considered the question and came up with something to appease Bailey. "You find out where Holly was every day and night this past week and do it in a way that doesn't ruffle any feathers."

Bailey took up the challenge. "I'll find out, but I can't promise all the feathers will be on the bird when I'm finished."

Fen returned to the table where Holly's grandfather and mom waited. "Are you two sure you don't want anything to drink?"

Both shook their heads. Cindi bothered a fingernail while sitting erect. Stony turned to her. "Relax. You look like a rabbit staring at a coyote."

She lowered her hand and allowed her shoulders to roll forward.

Fen needed to put her more at ease so he started talking. "Your father told me he came to spend the night in the cabin with you on Monday night. Tell me about the cabin."

She cut her eyes to her father and then spoke in a loud whisper. "It's very nice. I brought a bag of books I've been dying to read." She put her hand over her mouth. "I'm sorry. I didn't mean to say dying."

He gave her a smile intended to convey she'd done nothing wrong. "I know this is unsettling to you, but take a deep breath and let it out slowly. I promise this won't take long and you can get back to relaxing by the river."

Her chin dipped. "It's so peaceful there. The cabin has two

bedrooms, a lovely little kitchen, and the most delicious front porch overlooking the river."

"Did you cook for your father and Holly on Monday?"

"Daddy grilled steaks. All I did was make the salad and microwave the potatoes. I know they're better baked, but we didn't want to wait."

"Tell me what you've done the rest of the week."

"You're going to think I'm the most boring person you've ever met, but I only left the cabin once and that was to go to the grocery store. It was Tuesday morning, around ten o'clock."

"It sounds to me like you were ready for a vacation. Have you been on any hikes?"

"No. Just sitting on the porch, reading."

"That sounds wonderful. My late wife loved books. She also liked to move a lawn chair to the water's edge and put her feet in the water while she read. Have you dipped your toes in the river since you came to Kerrville?"

"No, I'm so fair-skinned I burn instead of tan. I'd need to cover up to sit by the river, but it sounds like a lovely idea."

So far, the conversation reminded Fen of a poorly written script to a boring movie. Time to shake things up. "Your father told me about Holly's birth father, Roger Slade. When was the last time you had any contact with him?"

At the sound of Roger Slade's name, Cindi shuddered. The question brought one hand over her heart and the other over her mouth. A blush of shame rose up her neck. Her gaze went immediately to her father.

She wasn't the only one to react. Stony's countenance changed from flesh to granite. "That's enough. We don't talk about him. Ever."

Cindi found her voice. "It's all right, Daddy. It just took me by surprise." She hooked her blond hair behind both ears and locked her gaze on Fen. "Mr. Maguire, I've had no contact with

Roger Slade since I was a senior in high school. He was the biggest mistake I ever made, but it resulted in a child that I couldn't be more proud of."

Stony stood and looked down at Fen. "We're finished here."

He nodded. "Yes, sir. I agree."

Fen stayed in the dining room, processing what he'd learned. He could almost taste the fear Cindi felt toward her father, strong enough that Roger Slade was nothing but a terrible memory. Was that true or a response she'd crafted over the years?

Bailey joined him. "Holly's mom and grandfather came and told her they were leaving. He didn't look happy."

His mouth engaged before his brain. "He's going to be less happy when he finds out Holly's mom is playing house with someone in the cabin by the river."

Bailey leaned forward. "She looks repressed enough to play a stay-at-home parent in an old television show. How do you know she's entertaining someone?"

"Whisker burns on her chin. She claims all she's done since coming to Kerrville is read, avoid the sun, and has only left the cabin once. Her chin tells a different story."

Bailey whistled. "I'd have never thought about whisker burns. Good catch. I'll remember to date guys who shave smooth or have full beards."

He ignored the last comment and focused on Cindi. "I'm not interested in her love life. It's her deception that has me wondering if there's not more to Cindi than meets the eye." He locked his gaze on Bailey. "Play nice, but see if you can find out what Holly's mother is like when Grandpa Stony isn't hovering over her. She's way too pretty for there not to be a man or two chasing her."

Bailey puffed out her cheeks. "I asked you to give me something to do. I wasn't expecting it to be this much."

"If you can't handle it—"

She cut him off. "I didn't say anything about not being able to do the job. It's just that I need to set up the booth tonight and load the paintings early in the morning. That doesn't leave much time to talk to Holly."

"You'll find a way."

Bailey leaned forward. "What will you be doing tomorrow?"

"Processing what Lou tells me tonight and what I learned today."

"Speaking of Lou. What's she doing?"

"Selling stories and expecting me to call her with the next big scoop."

Bailey stared at him. "I recognize that look. You're not calling her, are you?"

He stood. "She's busy, and I need to spend the rest of the day coaching young artists."

"Do you plan on stopping by the booth tomorrow?"

"It all depends on how my knee feels."

Bailey wiggled her eyebrows. "Stop by if you can. I may have a surprise for you."

Chapter Sixteen

By the time Fen made it to Mamacita's Mexican Restaurant, the line of people waiting for a table stretched out the door and down a sidewalk. He bypassed the people, most wearing summer shorts with sandals, and joined Lou near the front of the queue. Dagger stares came from a couple in their sixties sporting an array of turquoise and silver jewelry, who must have thought he was cutting line. It wasn't long before a hostess guided them to a seat in the corner of the main dining room. The room was made to look like the plaza of a Mexican or Spanish town, with stores lining the ground floor and fake residences above them, some complete with balconies.

"Great decor," said Fen. "If the food is half as good as the atmosphere, we're in for a treat."

"I need a stiff drink," said Lou. "It's been one heck of a day."

The server arrived and took drink orders of iced tea for him and a large frozen margarita for Lou.

He continued to admire the intricacies of the murals in the

pretend town as Lou asked, "Did you make any progress today?"

He brought his gaze down from a balcony, looked at her, and replied, "You look tired."

She leaned on her elbows. "Someone woke me very early this morning. By noon, I'd put in a full day and hadn't showered yet. I should have gone back to bed. The afternoon was a lot of wasted effort."

"Did you sell all the stories you wanted to?"

She put her elbows on the table. "I never sell as much as I believe I should, but I did all right. What about you? Did you have a productive day?"

"Like you, I divided my day into morning and afternoon. The first half was all about Jewell."

She interrupted him before he could tell her about his afternoon with students. "I need more details on her death than what Chief Strange and the mayor told me and what they said in their press conference."

Fen began with the first person to contact the police. "Do you know about the owner of a donut shop reporting something in the water by the park?"

Lou nodded. "I had to track him down. He made me promise I'd put the name of his shop in my story before he agreed to talk about it. It added a little human interest to the narrative, and I scored a free bear claw and a cup of coffee." She tilted her head. "What else?"

Fen started with the early morning knock on his door and talked until their drinks, chips, and salsa arrived. He added sugar to his tea as Lou started dipping chips in salsa. He picked up a chip and dipped it into the red salsa. He had one chip for every three of Lou's and wondered if she'd not eaten all day. She drank from a glass goblet that looked big enough to house several goldfish. The drinks and the pre-meal basket of chips were half gone when they resumed their conversation.

"Did you try to interview the two ex-husbands?" asked Fen.

Lou rolled her eyes upward and lowered her slush-filled glass. "That was this afternoon. If I'd gotten to them this morning I might have had a chance at an interview, or at least have seen their immediate reaction to Jewell's death. No such luck. Independent reporters came from far and wide like buzzards flocking to road kill. They cashed in on the video of Jewell's exes blaming each other."

"Sounds like you all had a flash-flood of prosperity."

"I should have scored both stories, but that's the way it is in my business. Feast or famine and not much in between." She took another drink of the frozen concoction and resettled the fishbowl-sized glass on the table. "I finally caught up with Jeremy Key as he was leaving the hotel around noon. By that time, he'd already shot off his mouth to another reporter. He told me to direct questions to his attorney."

"That answer never slowed you down before. Did he respond to anything?"

"I asked him if he was going to take over parenting Candice. He kept walking. I think he'd been crying."

She reached for the goblet again. "I stopped him in his tracks when I mentioned Cliff Rouse was still in town."

"That's more like it. How did he react?"

"As expected. He suggested the police start their investigation with husband number two."

"Were you able to speak to Mr. Rouse?"

"A reporter from San Antonio got to him this morning. He got some great footage of Cliff accusing Jeremy of killing her. His attorney must have spoken to him before I got to him about making accusations without proof. He told me to take a hike."

He watched droplets of condensation slide down his glass

of iced tea. "Jewell's in the morgue in San Antonio and they're still fighting over her. Do you know if any other ex-husbands are coming to join the brawl?"

"Reporters tracked down two others who said they'd be at the funeral. The last ex is out of the country on business. No word on him yet."

Lou took the straw that came with her drink and stirred the slush. "Your turn. How did Candice take the news? Did she cry?"

"Not for long. It started out with the typical stages of grief: shock, denial, unbelief, anger... you know. It took her less than a minute to zip through those and realize she's a very wealthy young lady. When she left me, she was going to her room to call her mother's attorney. My guess is she wanted to find out how rich she is."

Lou didn't hesitate. "Her mom's estimated net worth is in the neighborhood of seven million dollars."

"That a nice neighborhood," said Fen.

Lou nodded in agreement. "She clipped her exes for a million each and accumulated the rest from investments and gifts from male friends." Lou put air quotes on the word friends.

"Doesn't surprise me. According to Candice, Jewell had plans to remarry and divorce each of her exes to see what she could get out of them the second time around."

Lou shook her head in disbelief. "Was she that much of a woman, or are some men brainless?" Her eyes brightened. "That would have made a good tell-all book if she'd lived long enough to pull it off."

"Not bad," he said as he dipped another chip into the red sauce. "You could compare her to Jezebel in the Bible. She had King Ahab wrapped around her finger and was responsible for the deaths of many men." He stuffed the chip in and spoke after chewing. "I make it a rule to never underestimate women, especially the beautiful ones."

"Is Candice cut from the same bolt of satin as her mother?"

"I'm not sure." He watched two servers deliver heaping piles of sizzling fajitas to a nearby table as he continued his thought. "Candice is ambitious and has the looks that turn heads. I expect her to take those millions and grow them, but she doesn't give off the same animal vibe as her mother did."

He looked at Lou and quirked a smile. "Of course I could be totally wrong about her. She may plot her own ways to fleece her mom's exes before she moves on to new victims."

Their food arrived and the conversation took another break. Moans of satisfaction replaced words until both pushed their plates a few inches toward the center of the table. Fen was the first to speak. "Do you know if Ray-Ray is still in jail?"

Lou tilted her head. "I've heard nothing to the contrary. Why are you asking about him?"

A shake of the head preceded him saying, "This goofy brain of mine jumps from one thing to the next when I get into an investigation. I guess it's how I keep track of all the pieces on the chessboard."

The server came and cleared their plates and asked if they had room for dessert. Fen raised his hands in surrender and Lou shook her head. The young lady grinned. "The desserts are exceptional. Leave room next time."

Lou hadn't finished talking about the street musician under arrest for killing Rose Cunningham. "The only thing I know about Ray-Ray is that the judge set bail at one million dollars."

Fen folded his hands on top of the table. "At least he'll start out clean and sober when he's released."

"Don't you mean if he's released?"

"He'll be out of jail by the time we go back to Newman County."

"You sound confident of that, former Sheriff Maguire." She waited a few seconds for a response that didn't come. "There must be a reason for your optimism about Ray-Ray's future. What else do you know that I don't?"

"Did you do a full background check on the members of the Gilmore family?"

"I wouldn't call it as thorough as what the FBI might do if they were vetting for top-secret clearance, but I nosed around enough to where I could write a decent story about any of them."

"What about Stony's wife?"

"She died five years ago in a house fire when he was out of town."

"How was their marriage?"

"On the rocks. He was more married to his banks than his wife. No signs of another woman." Lou looked away and brought her gaze back to him. "You don't think he..."

"Sometimes I think too much. I spoke with all three generations today. Stony lives up to his name. He's one of the most overbearing fathers or grandfathers I've ever met. Cindi rebelled in high school and wound up with a baby. I believe she's rebelling again, but she has the advantage of age and wisdom this time."

"Another man?"

He nodded.

"My mind is reeling. I'm picturing Cindi taking a page out of Jewell's manual on how to manipulate men and talking someone into killing Jewell." She took a breath. "What about Holly?"

"I may be wrong, but I think sweet little Holly has a latent streak of her mother's rebellion in her that's about to break out. She and Cindi put on fronts to make everyone believe they're sugar and spice and everything nice. I'm thinking about all the dirty things Jewell did to all three in the Gilmore clan. That must have had a cumulative effect. Stony is transparent as glass. He hated Cindi's high school heartthrob and got rid of him. Cindi and Holly are much more opaque about their feelings than Grandpa Stony, but I'm not counting either of them out."

"You had quite a morning," said Lou. "What do you want me to do?"

"Dig deeper into all three, but don't spook them. No offense, but subtlety isn't your strongest asset. Bailey's in the perfect position to glean information, so I gave her the assignment of finding out what Holly and Cindi are really like. Stay in touch with her and give her pointers on how best to proceed."

The server returned with Fen's credit card and thanked them for coming. He added a generous tip and both he and Lou stood. They didn't speak again until they were in the parking lot. Lou dug in her purse for keys. "I'll get to work tonight on finding out about the Gilmore family. What about you?"

"Nothing tonight but icing my knee. It's well on the mend, but I was on it a long time today."

"What about tomorrow?"

"I want to act like a tourist and check out the craft booths. We should both stop by Bailey's booth to avoid disappointing her."

"Don't expect me to be there early. My internal alarm clock doesn't go off as early as yours."

He thought about spending most of the next day in the recliner, but that didn't appeal to him. Why not spend a few hours talking to customers? After all, half the paintings in the booth were his and people always enjoy talking to the artist. Bailey's mention of a surprise also intrigued him. She was up to something. Tomorrow could prove to be an interesting day.

Lou pressed the unlock feature on her car's key fob but

didn't reach for the door handle on her Camry. "Did Chief Strange make any progress on the case today?"

"I called him late this afternoon. Cops searched three miles upstream from the bridge. They picked up a lot of trash and took a lot of photos but found nothing of value. And no sign of a struggle."

"Did you tell him about your interviews with the Gilmore family?"

"I gave him the bare bones of what I told you without the speculation. He's under a ton of pressure from the mayor and city council. Facts are what he needs."

"Sounds like politics as usual." Lou climbed into her car. "See you later. It's time for me to get back to work."

Chapter Seventeen

It was approaching ten thirty the next morning when Fen parked between two white lines in the lot overlooking the park. A sea of white booths stood in the grass between him and the river. Somewhere before him was a booth filled with offerings by him and Bailey. He wondered again what she had up her sleeve.

The Chamber of Commerce couldn't have hoped for a more perfect day to host vendors selling their wares, including a large contingent of artists. Traffic stretched bumper-to-bumper on the bridge. If nothing else, Bailey should clean up today selling caricatures. She'd mastered the ability to pump out high-quality sketches of people that emphasized a physical characteristic in a humorous yet non-offensive way. Earlier in the year she got him to agree to charge half-price for children's caricatures. When she started training with him last fall, he insisted she do them for free.

He tested the gimpy knee and found it to be stable and pain-free. The ice he'd applied the previous night had done the trick. A strong elastic bandage to keep it from moving also helped.

"Time to find her," he said as he locked his truck.

He made it as far as the grass when a voice called out from behind him. "Hold up, Mr. Maguire."

Mindful not to make any sharp turns, he stopped and craned his neck. It was Mayor Fred Bean barreling toward him on short legs. Although the morning was cool, the mayor wiped his brow with a red bandanna.

"I'm delighted to see you up on your pegs again. You're not even limping."

"All the bits and pieces must have found their way back into place. When it pops out all I have to do is stay off it for several days and then it's good until I make too quick of a turn or the weather tells me it's going to rain." He pointed to the booths. "A good crowd is already here with plenty more people coming. I wasn't expecting so many vendors."

The mayor let out a noise that sounded like doubt. "Projections are for it to be down from last year. The talk of there being a mass killer has people spooked."

"A mass killer? Where in the world did that rumor start?"

Mayor Bean resembled a penguin as he waved his arms. "A radio station out of San Antonio found a professor to say he thought it could be a serial killer targeting beautiful women."

Fen shook his head. "There's a much better probability that the killer is someone the victims knew. That station is after ratings and the professor must be trying to sell a book. There's no telling where they dug up that so-called expert."

"That may be, but the members of the city council are having second thoughts about Ben Strange's ability to catch whoever killed Jewell."

He noticed the mayor didn't include Rose Cunningham's name. Better not remind him there were two murders to solve.

"I spoke with Ben last night and he's doing all that's possible. I know for a fact that his detectives have interviewed several potential suspects. There's no autopsy yet. All the evidence is being processed, and he's working day and night to gather information that I'm sure will lead to an arrest."

The mayor's eyebrows went up when he asked, "Does that mean you're still helping him?"

"Absolutely. As we speak, I have two associates in town. One is doing surveillance and the other is a research specialist developing a file of information a foot thick." The mayor didn't need to know that Lou might not be awake yet, and Bailey was likely drawing sketches of chubby-cheeked infants. All he wanted to hear was confirmation that Ben Strange's selection as chief of police wasn't a mistake he'd be blamed for.

"That somewhat eases my mind. At least I can put out a statement that says you're working with Ben and—"

Fen didn't let him finish. "Absolutely not! If you leak my name or the names of my associates, you'll blow our cover and possibly send the killer into hiding. Tell the press that Chief Strange has brought together a team that's making steady progress in their investigation. If they ask who, tell them the sheriff and state law enforcement."

The mayor nodded. "I won't have to bend the truth if I say that. I know for a fact that one of Jewell's ex-husbands talked to the governor and extracted a promise that state law enforcement would take over the case if progress stalled."

Fen put a hand on the mayor's shoulder and pointed with his other hand to the line of traffic coming across the bridge. "Look at all those people bringing business to your city." He brought his hands down. "I'll make a deal with you, Fred. If you'll act like this town is the safest place on earth, I'll do what I can to make it that way."

"By gum, you've got a deal! It's time for me to shake hands and welcome people to the safest city in the state."

The mayor turned, found the nearest person coming across the parking lot, and introduced himself. Fen turned as a wave of self-satisfaction put a bounce in his step. He'd bought time for himself and Ben to work on the case with little or no interference from the local politicians. His pace slacked when he realized the mayor wouldn't stay satisfied for long if another woman's body turned up in the river.

He didn't have to travel far before spotting his booth. Bailey had somehow scored a prime location and patrons lined up like she was giving away homemade ice cream. His eyes widened when Bailey walked out of the booth and stood behind Candice, who sat on a short stool with a sketch pad on an easel. His gaze shifted to the other corner of the front of the tent. Holly sat on an identical stool, drawing with swift, confident strokes.

Bailey looked up and motioned for him to hurry to her. She met him halfway. "Surprise!"

He wagged his head. "What in the world is going on?"

She leaned into him and whispered, "You told me to keep an eye on them so that's what I'm doing. I told them how much money I make at festivals like this by doing caricatures. Neither believed me so I challenged them to prove me wrong. They made a side bet to see who can earn the most money today. Candice is fast, but I'm having to make sure she doesn't rush too much." Her gaze shifted to the blond. "Holly wants to put in too much detail, so she's working on her speed. So far Candice is ahead but Holly's not far behind."

Fen couldn't help but issue a wry smile. He wondered if the competition might lead to hard feelings. "I'm glad to see you have them separated. I'd hate to see their rivalry break into a cat fight."

"No worries about that. The three of us had a long talk in my room last night. Holly was really sweet to Candice. She opened up about never having a father growing up. I told both of them about losing my dad when I was little. Candice said she didn't like it when her mother pulled all those nasty tricks on Holly and anyone else who posed a threat. She also described what it was like having a new stepfather every couple of years. It was awful, especially when they tried to tell her what to do."

Fen rubbed his chin. "Are you saying the rivalry was between the mothers and not the daughters?"

Bailey had her hair in a ponytail, which shook side to side. "You don't get it. The real rivalry was between Candice's mother and Holly's grandfather. Holly's mom doesn't cause waves, but that doesn't mean there aren't strong currents under the surface."

"That makes so much sense," said Fen. "I should have seen it before. Jewell was grooming Candice to live a life like hers. The same goes for the plans Stony has for Holly." He didn't say it but Stony moved up a space or two on the list of suspects.

"What else did you three talk about?"

"Everything. Holly had a six-pack in an ice chest in the trunk of her car. We used a rope to lift the cooler up through a window in my room. That gave us two each, just enough to loosen us up."

Fen groaned. "Please tell me Mrs. Dillworth didn't catch you."

Bailey rolled her eyes. "Even if that snoopy old woman had walked in on us, we had it covered. Pour it in an empty Starbucks cup and put a lid on it." She grinned. "McDonald's cups work just as good. It's all part of growing up on the streets of Houston."

Fen thought back to his youth and had to admit he was just as guilty as Bailey, even though he wasn't as careful about hiding it. Considering the fact that one girl had lost her mother, it wasn't worth pursuing underage drinking. Instead he changed the subject. "How are sales?"

A huge grin paved the way for her good news. "I sold one of yours the first thing to a man who didn't quibble over the price."

"Did you get his name?"

She nodded. "He never said over two words. He made one pass around the booth, picked out the painting you did of the Angelina River, and handed me his credit card. After the sale, he gave me his business card, took the painting, and left."

She reached into the back pocket of her jeans. Fen examined the card that read ALTON BROWN, JUSTICE OF THE PEACE.

His gaze went back to Bailey. "That's P.B.'s father."

"She's weird."

He looked over her shoulder into the booth. "What do you know about that? It goes to show you never know who your next customer is going to be."

Bailey put her hands on her hips. "You didn't ask about my sales." She continued without giving him a chance to answer. "Three paintings so far. One of wood ducks with wings cupped coming into a pond, the one of whitetail deer in a field, and the still life of the vase of flowers you told me to paint."

He tilted his head. "Isn't that the one you said no one in their right mind would ever buy?"

"Don't gloat. I'm still not satisfied with how it turned out."

Fen and Bailey went inside the booth where Bailey announced, "Ladies and gentlemen." She waited until all heads turned. "I'd like to introduce you to Mr. Fen Maguire. He's a nationally known and respected artist whose works are on the top row of the display. My name is Bailey Madison and I'm studying under his guidance. My works are displayed under his. Please ask us anything you wish."

The people didn't need to be asked twice. An hour later, Fen and Bailey had sold another painting each and Bailey had picked up a commission to paint a mother and child portrait. She was taking photos of the two when harsh voices crashed through the opening in the tent's front.

Fen took steps toward the opening and heard, "Get away from me. Neither of you are my father!"

Chapter Eighteen

A semicircle of people had gathered by the time Fen stepped out of the tent and into the sunshine. They focused on two men who'd squared off in front of Candice's easel with fists clenched and faces red with rage. Although he had never met them, he recognized them by the photos Lou had gathered of the potential murder suspects. On the left stood the man who claimed to be Candice's father, Jeremy. He wasn't a large man but looked as though he could hold his own if push came to shove. His jaw boasted a scrape, as did the knuckles on his right hand. Fen deduced these were the souvenirs of the recent bar fight at the Y.O. Hotel.

Opposite him, with feet set shoulder-length apart, stood a larger man with medical tape on the top corner of his left eyebrow. He had the advantage of weight carried around his midsection but looked to be several years older. It was Jewell's second husband, Cliff Rouse.

"I'm her father," shouted Jeremy. "I say what's good for Candice, not some slimy used-car dealer."

"New cars, and my net worth puts yours to shame." He

pointed with a stubby index finger. "You abandoned Candice when she was a baby, just like you left Jewell high and dry. I was Candice's real father and never quit paying child support, even though I didn't have to."

Before Fen could take a step forward, Bailey shot past him. "You two get out of here and leave Candice alone."

Holly was already on her feet and shouted, "You heard her! Candice doesn't want either of you in her life."

"Mind your own business," shouted Jeremy.

"This is my business," said Bailey. "I paid for this booth and you're not welcome here."

"Shut up, little girl," said Cliff Rouse.

Fen moved toward the fray but couldn't get past the three girls who stood shoulder to shoulder. He managed to yell over Bailey's head. "Everyone needs to step back and calm down." He should have saved his words for all the good they did.

The two men circled each other with nostrils flared and hands coming up in a fighting position. Jeremy shouted again. "If you think you can take my place as Candice's father you'd better think again." He kept his eyes on his opponent, but spoke out of the corner of his mouth. "Candice, you're coming with me."

"Like heck I am. If either of you clowns thinks you can tell me what to do, you'd better go back to school."

Cliff Rouse shook with rage. "Now look what you've done. You're nothing but poison to her, just like the oil you pump out of the ground. All you do is pollute the air, water, and land. Poison! That's what you are. I will not let you ruin Candice's life. I promised Jewell and I intend to keep my promise." His glare intensified. "Besides that, you killed her. For that, you don't deserve to live."

Both men swung at the same time and connected with similar results. The right cross by Cliff sent Jeremy careening into Bailey, who staggered back into Fen with enough force to send him reeling backward. Jeremy hit Cliff square on the bandage and spun him in a full circle.

When Fen looked up, Bailey was on his lap while both men were shaking off the effects of the first blow.

Blood trickled down the pugilists's faces as Fen checked his gimpy knee for damage. No streaks of pain shot up his leg, but he wasn't in a hurry to get to his feet. So far, so good. Best to stay down and watch.

Bailey was quick as a cat to bounce up, but by the time she got back in the fight, Candice had mounted her father's back and was pounding on his ear. She looked like a bull rider with her right arm flailing.

Holly hadn't stood by idly. She'd clawed furrows in Cliff Rouse's face. He thrust her aside with a left arm. This sent Holly sprawling into Bailey. It was a repeat of Bailey flying backward, tripping, and landing once again on Fen. Luckily, she didn't land on his bad knee.

She tried to pull her legs under her but Fen grabbed her wrist and didn't let go. Her bloody nose and glare told him she intended to do damage to both men. In a calm voice he said, "It's safer away from the fray. Go get Candice and Holly and tell them to come here. Let those two fools fight it out."

Bailey got to Holly first. She was attempting to get off the ground when she saw blood streaming from Bailey's nose. Her hand went over her mouth. Bailey grabbed her arm. "Let's get Candice away from them before she gets hurt."

Holly nodded and the two moved with quick steps as Jeremy spun and threw the would-be bull rider from his back. Bailey and Holly each took an arm and pulled until Candice was even with Fen. She looked down and gasped. "Are you all right?"

He nodded. "Better than Bailey." He reached into his back

pocket and took out a bandanna and spoke in a firm voice as he handed it to Bailey. "Ladies, you're staying here while those two idiots try to send each other to the hospital."

The three girls looked at each other and laughed. It was at that moment Fen knew something had bonded between the three that would last. They made bets without money about which of Jewell's ex-husbands would emerge the victor. The two men rolled in front of them, gouging, biting, and panting like parched dogs. By the time Ben Strange arrived with two officers, the men were so spent they couldn't do any more damage if they wanted to.

Bailey stemmed the flow of blood and washed her face with the water she'd brought. Somehow, she'd managed not to get any blood on her T-shirt or shorts.

Ben shook his head as he instructed his officers to hand-cuff Jeremy and Cliff. "Don't say I didn't warn you." He looked at his officers. "Book them for disturbing the peace and make sure they stay separated. Do everything by the book."

Ben looked down at Fen. "I'll need a witness statement from you."

"No problem. I had a front-row seat to everything."

A familiar voice came from behind. "You weren't the only one with a good view. This will make a great follow-up story to Jewell's murder." Lou stood over his shoulder, smiling.

He looked at Ben. "There's four strong women looking at me and none are offering to help get me on my feet."

Lou hooked her hands under his arms as Bailey and Candice each grabbed a hand. Between the three of them, they had him on his feet in no time. After thanking them, he looked at Candice and Holly. "Why don't you two take a break and get something to eat?"

"What about me?" asked Bailey. "I'm starving."

"Let her go with them," said Lou. "I'll stay with you and sell Bailey's paintings."

"Sell mine while you're at it." Fen looked at the families lining up for caricatures. "Looks like I'll be busy until you ladies get back from lunch."

Ben looked at Bailey. "Are you sure you're all right?"

She flipped the question aside. "This isn't my first bloody nose. Brings back memories of my childhood."

The police chief looked at the three young women. "If you girls like barbecue, I can take you to the vendor that has the best I've ever had."

Candice's dark eyes came alive. "My treat. I've been smelling the smoke for the last hour."

The three artists and the chief of police made their way through the crowd and were gone. Fen picked up Candice's stool, gathered her scattered pencils, and put the easel upright. He finished tearing off the top page of the sketch pad, which was not only ripped, but stained. He faced the crowd and spoke in a voice that sounded like a carnival barker. "Who's next for a free souvenir of your day in Kerrville?"

A teen with blue hair said, "The sign says twenty dollars for adults and ten for children under twelve."

Fen pulled the sign down. "It's your lucky day. Children are free until the other artists return and everyone else is half price."

"I'm not sure it's worth it."

"Too bad. If you were under ten, you'd get a free sketch."

"Uh... I'll be ten next week." The lie crossed her lips without her blinking or looking down.

"Let me see your driver's license."

She reached for her back pocket before thinking.

The corner of his lip pulled up. "I tell you what. Ten bucks and I'll use three colors."

"All right, but it better be good."

Lou whispered to him. "When the girls get back, I want to talk to you. I've been busy this morning. I may have found something."

Fen wished she hadn't teased him with something that might help him solve the case. Now he'd wonder what it was as he tried to concentrate on whipping out as many caricatures as possible while infusing them with humor and exaggerated details.

After about forty-five minutes, the three new best friends returned with one person extra joining them. It was the yoga instructor, Roy, walking between Candice and Holly. Fen took a good look and thought about how he might sketch him with undersized legs and head but a massive torso and arms.

Roy bid the girls good-bye without coming into the booth and disappeared into the crowd.

"How was the barbecue?" he asked.

"Outstanding," said Bailey. "Thelma's baked brisket is good, but there's nothing like beef cooked low and slow over a mesquite fire."

"I had burnt ends," said Holly.

Candice added, "Pork ribs for me. They almost fell off the bone."

Lou came from the tent. "Now I can't decide if I want beef brisket or pork ribs."

Fen raised himself from the stool. "Candice, I believe this is your workplace. You'd better get to work if you're going to beat Holly."

A mischievous grin came into Holly's smile. "No way. This is my day to win and I'm going to rub it in over supper tonight."

It was Bailey's turn to stoke the fire of competition. "I'm going to sell more of my paintings than both of you combined."

Holly and Candice grinned at each other. Candice was the

first to speak. "She talks big, but we can take her." Holly nodded her partial agreement. "First we'll beat Bailey and then I'll beat you. Two victories for me in one day."

Fen interrupted. "No one will win anything if you stand here talking while customers are waiting."

That was all it took. Bailey scurried into the tent while Candice and Holly took up their positions outside. Lou handed Holly a tube of sunblock. "Candice looks like she tans without trying, but you'll need this. Your arms are already pink."

Holly took the tube and began slathering it on. "It's a good thing there's trees and shade. Mom's always getting on me about staying out of the sun."

Fen listened as Lou continued, "Speaking of your mom. Is she coming today?"

Holly raised her shoulders and let them drop. "I'm surprised she hasn't shown up yet. I talked to her last night. She was out of breath and seemed distracted."

Fen dipped into the conversation. "Oh? Was she working out?"

Holly shook her head. "Mom's idea of working out is finding her purse before she goes shopping. I don't know what's going on with her. Her and Grandpa are coming to the booth, but she didn't say when. She might have said they had a meeting this morning at the branch bank here in town. I don't always listen as closely as I should."

Lou waited until they were well away from the booth. "What was all that about?" she asked.

"All what?"

"Don't play dumb. You were pumping Holly for information about her mom. What did you hear that went right over my head?"

A smile crept onto Fen's face. "You've been married three times. Ever get out of breath and distracted at night?"

Lou rolled her eyes. "How dumb can I be?" She cut her eyes his way. "Who do you think the distraction is?"

He shrugged. "I don't have a clue." He kept walking. "Your turn. What can you tell me about Stony?"

"Like I told you earlier, I've been busy. It seems Stony is very much made of flesh, bone, and clogged arteries. His heart and brain are a ticking time bomb."

Fen acknowledged the information with a nod and said, "Doesn't surprise me. Stress can rob a person of so much life. He's trying to live three lives at once: his own, his daughter Cindi's, and Holly's."

"I don't get it," said Lou. "His reputation in the banking community is spotless. He runs a tight ship and his employees speak well of him, even that he's generous to a fault if you're loyal."

They walked on and took in the displays of all manner of items offered by the vendors, but Fen's mind was fixed on Stony. He stopped at the end of a line of booths. "I think Stony is one of those men who does many things exceptionally well. His downfall comes in knowing what to do with his own family."

"That's very perceptive." Lou pulled out her phone. "The housefire that killed his wife probably saved him the embarrassment of a divorce."

"Did you find out anything interesting about Cindi or Holly?"

"Not much about Holly, but her mother is showing signs of wanting out from under Stony's thumb. He gave her a branch to run and word is that she sometimes comes into work a little bleary-eyed."

Fen looked at the lake while the seed of a thought sprouted in his brain. "What do you think about Bailey, Candice, and Holly paying Cindi an unannounced visit?"

Lou shook her head. "I like the idea of an unannounced visit, but I want to do it."

"Why not the three amigos? After today those three are going to be thick as cold oatmeal."

"Nice metaphor but you're not thinking of Bailey."

"Of course I'm thinking of her. She's a tremendous asset. Why not use her? Besides, she loves undercover work."

Lou tapped her index finger on her temple. "Think, Fen. How many friends does Bailey have?"

"Uh... If you count Holly and Candice, that makes two."

"Exactly. She'll have none if Holly or Candice find out Bailey is trying to find evidence that could implicate Holly's mom in Jewell's murder."

Fen tilted his head. "Do you think Cindi killed Jewell?"

"She's my second choice. The first is someone she talked into doing it for her." Lou took a step toward him. "Under the surface Cindi is a very smart and calculating woman. She had years to study Jewell and the way she manipulated men into doing whatever she wanted them to do. With all that training, I believe she hatched her own plan to get rid of Jewell. All she needed was a man she could manipulate."

Instead of responding Fen lifted his head and sniffed the air. "Unless I'm mistaken, we're close to the food vendors. I wonder if they have barbecue chicken."

Lou stomped her foot. "You can be so aggravating it makes my teeth itch. I gave you a perfect solution to Jewell's murder and you ignored it."

"Not true. I'm thinking about what you said and all the pieces don't fit."

"Like what?"

He tapped his temple with his index finger. "Think. When you have the answer, we'll discuss it more. Until then, neither of us can expect to solve anything on an empty stomach."

Chapter Nineteen

I t was a quiet lunch and walk back to the booth, which was fine with Fen. Talking to customers, watching a fistfight, seeing three budding artists join as friends, and having Lou mad at him was enough sensory input for one day. Not many of the morning's events had anything to do with solving two murders. He needed to tell Lou she'd done a good job discovering Stony Gilmore's physical problems.

He turned to her. "Thanks for the information on Stony. You'd have made an excellent homicide detective."

She responded with a snort.

"I've been thinking. You might be right about Cindi talking someone into killing Jewell."

Lou cut her eyes toward him. "You don't believe that."

"I said it's possible. It's also possible that Cindi and her father planned it out together. He's a shrewd old buzzard or he wouldn't own all those banks. The more I ponder this case the more complicated it gets. Try this on for size: Cindi and Stony get a belly full of Jewell rigging contests. Stony hires someone." He paused. "No. He enlists someone who owes him a big favor. That someone isn't a pro and mistakes Rose Cunningham for Jewell. They get it right the second time around."

Lou looked at him full on. "You're probably the only person who still thinks about Rose Cunningham."

"I'm sure her family does." He pointed toward town. "Don't forget about Ray-Ray who's still in jail for a crime someone else almost certainly committed."

Fen held up his hand with fingers spread. "Of course, there's still five ex-husbands to consider. Every one of them has enough money and contacts to have someone killed. What if one of them found out about Jewell's plan to run back through the list of exes and take them for another million each? What if that fist-fight today was staged? Who knows? All five might have conspired to do her in. Can you imagine trying to unravel that mess? The state's top lawyers would defend them and drag the case out until me and you are living down the hall from each other in a nursing home."

Lou reeled back. "I could've done without that mental image." She took a step forward. "You win. I can see why you told me to think. We're far from solving this."

They fell into step side by side. "Don't look so disheartened. We're getting closer. You were right about not sending Bailey to snoop on Cindi but someone needs to. How would you like to take care of that? Get names of any boyfriends she's had in the last ten years. See if she cast a spell on any of them the way Jewell did with so many men."

"Sounds like fun. I have a natural distrust of women who allow their fathers to control their lives."

"Thank you," said Fen and he meant it.

The next surprise of the day came as they rounded the corner leading to Fen's booth. He spied Cindi standing behind Holly, watching her sketch a young couple. Holly burst out in a wide grin when he and Lou approached. "This is Clay and Kristin. They got married yesterday."

"Congratulations! I can't think of a better remembrance of your honeymoon than one of Holly's works. Make sure she signs it. One day, that signature may be worth more money than you can count."

Fen turned his attention to Cindi. "Come to see your daughter earning a little pocket change?"

Cindi spoke in a soft voice. "I wasn't expecting this to be such a lucrative hobby." She lowered her voice. "I also wasn't expecting Holly and Candice to be locked in such a fierce, friendly competition." She cut her eyes toward Holly's long-time rival. "I'm having a hard time believing what I'm seeing."

Fen took her by the arm and led her away. "Don't worry about either of them winning. It's a three-way bet regarding who will have the most sales. Bailey's selling her acrylic paint-ings. She had four grand worth of sales before we went to lunch."

He stepped back. "Where are my manners? This is Lou Cunningham, author and part-time reporter. She's here to cover the competition."

Lou took over. "I'm here to write a piece for an art maga-zine. I'm hoping to interview some parents of the top competi-tors. Of course Holly's name came up and here we are together. How fortuitous. Do you have a few minutes?"

"Well... I guess so. My father is on his way so I can't talk very long."

"Great. Let's take a walk. I can't think with this many people around."

Fen turned to Holly and gave her a suggestion to exaggerate the look of fear on the groom's face as the bride chased him toward a church. Otherwise the sketch was ready to sign and she could move on to her next client. He moved to check on

Candice as she finished another sketch and collected a cash payment. "How are you holding up?"

"Good." She paused. "Not great, but good. Losing Mom is just now sinking in. I keep expecting her to show up with some new man. It's weird knowing I'm all alone now."

"I've heard it said that as long as you have friends, you're never alone."

Candice shot a glance toward her former rival. "Don't tell anyone, but I'm hoping I can talk Holly into being my roommate when we go to college. Do you think her mom will give her grief about it?"

Words flowed without him over-thinking the question. "Holly's mom impresses me as a reasonable woman."

"Yeah, but what about Holly's grandfather? He's a tough old bird."

He couldn't deny her assessment of Stony. Advice should have come from him, but he sensed that whatever he said wouldn't be adequate. He settled for, "Concentrate on your sketches for the rest of the afternoon. Then get cleaned up and go out for a nice supper. Make plans to do something fun after the competition is over."

"We're not waiting that long. Holly and I are going to the Coming King Sculpture Prayer Garden tomorrow morning. I wish Bailey could come with us, but she said she needed to work the booth."

Fen rubbed his chin. "Sunday mornings are always slow. I'll work the booth tomorrow and she can have the whole day off if she needs it. We don't have to do caricatures."

"Awesome!" She motioned for the next customer to take a seat. That was his cue to check on Bailey and get to work.

Bailey met his arrival by announcing, "Attention, everyone. This is Fen Maguire. His paintings are on the top row. It's his turn to talk while I give my voice a break. He'll be glad to answer all your questions."

The patrons chuckled but took Bailey's words to heart and lined up. He walked to the left corner of the booth and stood with his hand extended to the first painting. "This is a good representation of my work. I specialize in landscapes, especially Texas landscapes. If you have questions about any of the works, please stand in front of the painting and I'll be around to talk to you about it."

A woman spoke up. "I don't need to talk. I want to buy."

"You're my favorite kind of customer. Bailey will take it down for you, wrap it, and run your credit card."

For the next thirty minutes, he worked his way around the booth and sold one of Bailey's works to a customer who preferred one of his oils but had a budget for an acrylic. He sealed the deal by saying, "One way of collecting art is to find a promising young artist, purchase one of their early works, and watch it go up in value. Bailey Madison is a rising star in the art world. You'll be glad you got one of her works at this amazing price."

The couple agreed to the purchase and Bailey took over. As she ran the credit card, a loud voice came from outside the tent. He wondered what kind of drama was playing out now. Hadn't there been enough excitement for one day?

"Don't argue with me, young lady. I said get yourself up and come with me." The bellowing voice came from Stony.

Holly didn't budge. "You don't understand, Grandpa."

"I have eyes, don't I? You should be working on your painting for the competition." He cut his gaze toward Candice. "Don't you see? This is one of her mother's schemes to distract you."

"That's not true," said Holly, as her chin quivered like she'd caught a chill.

Bailey came to Holly's defense. "That's right, Mr. Gilmore. This was my idea. Neither Candice nor her mom had anything to do with it."

He pointed to Bailey with a shaky finger. "You back off, young lady. This is family business."

Bailey stood her ground. "No, sir, this is my business. I rented this space. Holly and Candice agreed to work today and you're interfering with my livelihood."

Fen groaned and moved to quell the disturbance. Stony spun to face him. His face looked the color of a pink rose. "Maguire, you'd better put a leash on your girl and tell her to shut her big mouth."

The words made Fen bristle but he tamped down his desire to respond in anger. It was then he noticed Cindi and Lou running toward them. Cindi spoke before she arrived beside Holly. For once she spoke in a voice that commanded attention. "Holly, what's wrong?"

Stony directed his attention to his daughter. "Did you know about this?"

"About what?"

"About Holly wasting her time drawing cartoons with that woman's daughter."

Cindi placed her hands on her hips. "I didn't know about it until today but I think it's wonderful."

Fen looked at Stony and pictured a character with smoke coming from his ears. It seemed Cindi had found her spine and might be on the verge of a life-changing event. Better to keep his mouth shut and see how things played out.

"Wonderful?" shouted Stony. "What do you know about dealing with people like that girl over there? You thought Roger Slade was a wonderful boy, and look where that got you."

Cindi didn't back down. Her voice intensified. "I'll tell you what it got me... a wonderful, compassionate, and talented daughter."

"If she's so good, she'd show respect to me and do as I tell her. You've spoiled that child rotten."

Holly found her voice. "That's not true, Grandpa. Mom trusts me to decide some things on my own. We talk about things and we listen to each other."

"You're not old enough to make important decisions on your own." He glared at his granddaughter. "If she's such a wonderful mother, she'd have taught you not to talk back." His glare came through narrowed eyelids. "You're leaving with me, and I mean now."

Cindi took a half step forward. "She's leaving when she's finished her commitment to work. You're the one who drilled that into me." She deepened her voice to mimic her father. "Be the first to arrive at work and the last to leave."

Fen glanced over at Candice, who had her head in her hands with shoulders rising and falling as sobs poured out. Cindi noticed the effect on Candice and glared at her father. "That girl lost her mother yesterday and all you can think about is some silly competition. Can't you see what you're doing?"

The color changed in Stony's face from pink to crimson. "I'm protecting my family from a scheming woman who's reaching out from the grave to take my granddaughter from me."

Holly cast her gaze toward Candice and noticed her sobbing. She shot from her stool, went to her friend, and gathered her in her arms.

"See?" shouted Stony. "That proves it. Jewell's plan is playing out in front of your eyes." He took a gasping breath. "I will not tell you again." He grabbed his left arm with his right and repeated, "I will not tell you..."

Fen took three quick steps and caught Stony before he slumped to the ground. "Call EMS."

Lou was already reaching for her phone.

The words "Father" and "Granddad" came from Cindi and Holly as they kneeled beside the fallen patriarch. Fen checked for a pulse. Nothing. He placed his hand on Stony's chest, hoping to feel a rise and fall. Again, nothing.

A woman came forward. "I'm a nurse."

"No pulse or breathing," said Fen.

"We need to start CPR."

Lou nudged Fen out of the way and breathed air into the body until first responders came from the first aid tent. They shocked Stony with a portable defibrillator but their eyes told the story their words didn't. An ambulance crew soon arrived and life-saving procedures continued. Fen had seen this macabre scene play out many times as a highway patrol officer and as sheriff. EMTs would continue life-saving measurers until they could get the patient to the hospital and allow a medical doctor to pronounce death. It cut down on paperwork and lawsuits, and got things back to normal in short order. The downside was, it kept false hope alive for a while longer.

Chapter Twenty

Fen knew Bailey wanted to go to the hospital even before she asked. He took Cindi's shaking hand. "You're in no condition to drive. Bailey will drive you and Holly."

Cindi looked at Holly, who was wiping tears with the back of her hand and nodding. "He's right, Mom. We're both so upset it wouldn't be safe."

Bailey turned to Candice. "Follow us."

Candice responded with a nod.

The ambulance crew pulled close enough to the end of the row that they didn't have far to go before loading the motorized stretcher carrying Stony. Fen pulled Bailey aside as she grabbed her purse from inside the tent. "If you can't get behind the ambulance, there's no reason to get in a big hurry. He's gone."

Bailey dipped her head. "I understand, and I'll be careful."

The crowd soon dispersed, as did the line of people waiting to have sketches done or inquire about paintings. Fen turned to Lou. "Can you stick around? Someone needs to stay with the paintings while I take over out here."

Lou looked at the near-empty aisle before them. "The vibe

sure changed. I may have to have another margarita tonight to get off this emotional roller coaster."

Fen tried to lighten the mood. "I thought you newshounds couldn't get enough action and raw emotion."

"Up to a point. It's different when you've done research on someone then you watch him drop dead in front of you. It's a crying shame that the last conversation Cindi and Holly had with him was so acrimonious. They say you always remember a person's last words."

Fen didn't have time to respond as a grim-faced mayor and Chief Strange walked up. As usual, the mayor spoke first. "There's been more activity in this booth today than the city council is comfortable with. First a fist-fight resulted in two prominent men being arrested, and now Stony Gilmore is being rushed to the hospital. I heard a rumor it's because of another altercation. Is that right?"

He looked at the mayor and then at Ben Strange, who dipped his head. Fen hooked his thumbs in the front pockets of his jeans and looked straight into the mayor's beady left eye. "Why don't you stop beating around the bush and say what you came to say?"

The mayor held up his hands as stop signs. "Don't shoot the messengers. The members of the city council believe both situations could have been handled in a more diplomatic way. Furthermore, they said, er..."

He seemed to search for words so Fen helped him. "Cut to the chase. I'm to shut down my booth."

"I wouldn't put it so bluntly but..."

Fen took two steps toward him and whispered, "All you had to do was ask." He stepped back. "I'll even go one better to appease the city council, but it comes with one condition. You tell them Chief Strange convinced me to pack up immediately and not reopen until next weekend. That should satisfy the city council." He paused and gave the mayor his best hard stare. "It should also satisfy anyone else who has a problem with me."

The pointed words caused the mayor's second chin to wobble as he swallowed. He choked out. "That's mighty good of you, Mr. Maguire. I'll let the council know what we agreed to."

"Not we," said Fen with a firm voice. "The agreement is between me and Chief Strange. Believe me, you and the city council had nothing to do with my decision."

"Of course. My mistake."

"One more thing," said Fen. "I'm sure the city council and the district attorney know that Raymond Ray was in jail when someone else killed Jewel."

"Who was in jail?"

Ben spoke up. "Ray-Ray."

The mayor tilted his head. "I think everyone in town knows he's in jail for killing that Cunningham woman from San Antonio. It seems like an open and shut case."

Fen pulled a hand down his face. "The only evidence I've heard is that he had her credit cards on him. He admits that those came from Rose Cunningham's purse. A purse that was found a hundred yards upstream from the body."

The mayor must have sensed something might be amiss because he turned to Ben. "I thought this was an airtight case."

Ben shook his head. "It got a lot weaker when the DNA results from Ray-Ray's clothes, hands, and under his fingernails came back. There's nothing to show he ever touched the victim."

"He must have cleaned up in the river."

Chief Strange shook his head. "If you'd smelled Ray-Ray when we took him in, you'd know he hadn't cleaned up in quite a while."

Fen added, "There's another inconvenient fact. He was

sleeping off enough wine and barbiturates on the far bank to make him harmless as a kitten. I'm wondering how long it will be before his attorney demands a reduction in bail. It's possible there could be a lawsuit for false arrest."

"How do you figure that?"

"He never used the credit cards or spent the cash. Ray-Ray could claim he found them and was too drunk to turn them in until he sobered up."

Red-faced and at a loss for words, the mayor turned and waddled off to take care of other duties. At least now he had something else to worry about.

Behind his back Fen heard hand claps, and turned to see Lou smiling as she brought her hands together again. "Masterfully done, Fen. No one but you, me, and Chief Strange need to know that you wanted to close the booth early today and not work it tomorrow. You also gave the mayor a good kick in the pants without him knowing it."

Ben Strange extended his hand. "Every time I think the mayor has me by the scruff of my neck, you turn it around on him. I'm not sure how I can make it up to you."

Fen didn't have to think as his gaze shifted to the booth over his shoulder. "We'll call it even if you get me some help to take this down and haul it to my truck. There're still two murders to solve and things are more difficult now that we're down one source of information. Stony was a person who might have had answers but he died right where you're standing."

Ben looked down and back up. "Don't count him out yet. They broadcast on the way to the hospital that he might have a pulse."

Fen shook his head twice. "That's a story like the mayor saying the city council sent you two. They don't meet without public notice given first unless it's a genuine emergency. Shutting down a booth at a weekend fair doesn't qualify."

"Point taken," said Ben. "Officer Craven is on a quad bike with a dump bed. There are also city maintenance workers I can wrangle into helping you. They'll get you packed up and out of here in no time."

Ben keyed his radio and put the plan in motion. All Fen had to do was supervise, which suited him fine. Lou had been around him long enough to know how the paintings fit in the racks in the back of his truck, so she oversaw the loading in the parking lot. In less than half an hour, there was no sign the booth had ever been there. It occurred to him how quickly things can change. The difference between life and death for Stony was mere seconds.

With the tent folded and loaded onto the trailer, Fen joined Officer Craven in the quad bike. The officer spoke as they drove. "It's a shame about Mr. Gilmore. Doc Hargrove pronounced him dead within five minutes of arrival."

Fen nodded. "At least death came quick. When it's my time, that's how I'd prefer to go."

"Speaking of death," said the skinny officer. "How're the murder investigations going?" He dodged a large rock. The deputy cocked his head, hesitating before he said, "Tell me if that's none of my business."

Fen cast a glance at the young officer. Something about his inquisitiveness struck a chord. "We're chipping away at things, but I sense I'm missing something. Do you have any theories?"

"The word going around is that the autopsy showed the latest victim had her throat crushed with a metal pipe."

Fen nodded. "That's what Chief Strange told me. Any ideas on that?"

"Not really, but I haven't sat down with a pen and paper and made a list of possibilities. There are lots of types of pipes."

They were nearing his truck when Fen said, "Thanks for

the ride and even more for giving me something to do tomorrow."

"What's that?"

"I'm going to find out the diameter of the pipe used to kill Jewell, sit in my recliner, and make a list of every type of pipe I can think of that might make a suitable weapon in this scenario."

"I'll do the same if you want me to. I do a little welding and know something about construction. Give me your email address and I'll send it to you."

"Come by my place and we'll compare lists." He extended a hand and received a firm handshake. "Thanks for helping with the booth and paintings."

"All part of being a cop. It might be Monday before I can get that list to you. I'm working a double shift tomorrow."

"No problem. Tomorrow's going to be my paint-and-think day."

Lou closed the rear door of Fen's quad-cab truck and met him as she stepped to the driver's door. "I had to put most of Bailey's paintings in the back seat. Ever since she decked out her SUV with racks, you two carry twice as many paintings to sell."

"Ride with me. We'll go to the university and put hers back in the art studio."

"Don't you want me to follow you?"

"You can if you want to, but this parking lot is only a couple of blocks out of my way going back to my condo. Besides, I need you to tell me what you learned from Cindi when you took her for a walk."

He had the air conditioner blowing at full force as they joined a caravan of vehicles inching across the bridge. Once they reached the first stoplight on the north side of the bridge, they turned right and evaded most of the traffic, which was headed toward the interstate. The air conditioner hit its stride and brought relief.

"That's much better," said Lou as she dabbed her forehead with a tissue. "It was a cool enough morning, but the afternoon is making up for it."

Fen's mind barely registered her words. Instead of the weather, his thoughts were a jumble of faces, names, and memories of threats, fights, and deaths. He pushed them aside and focused on gathering more information. "You and Cindi were gone for quite a while. What did you learn?"

"We talked about vacations."

Fen shot her a quick glance. "Vacations?"

A mischievous smile had parted Lou's lips. "You can learn a lot about a person by asking them where they've gone on vacation and where they'd like to go. I broke the ice by telling her how many times I went to Vegas with my three husbands before they were ex-husbands." She turned toward him. "Now that I think about it, you'd have thought I learned my lesson about men who liked to gamble and go to risqué shows. Have you ever been to Vegas?"

"Once. I flew there, picked up a prisoner wanted for voluntary manslaughter, and flew back. It was an early flight out of Austin and a late flight back. All in all, a miserable trip."

"It didn't tempt you to see the sights or the long-legged women wearing little more than sequins and a smile?"

"Nope. Sally was five nine. She had all the legs I could ever want." He let out a sigh and said, "Get back to explaining to me what Cindi's vacations have to do with two murders."

"It's not only where she goes on vacation, it's who goes with her and who is there. My investigation isn't complete, but I sense I'm on to something."

Fen nodded that he was tracking.

"Stony kept a short leash on Cindi after she got pregnant in high school. In fact, she lived with Stony and his wife until Mrs. Gilmore had enough of him and talked about leaving. Stony put Cindi in charge of one of the branch banks shortly after that."

"How old was Holly when her grandmother died?"

"Twelve." Lou pulled her seat belt away from her chest and twisted a little more to face him. "This is all from my previous research. I'll let you know when I get to the new information."

She seemed to collect her thoughts and continued. "Stony was busy building and maintaining his empire, but he was on the verge of losing Holly's full-time caregiver and chauffeur, his wife. At the same time, they diagnosed him with a slew of physical problems. The doctor told him he'd need to do whatever it took to reduce the stress in his life or else."

Lou stopped talking as a car passed in a no-passing zone.

"I saw him coming," said Fen. "Keep going with your story."

Lou nodded and seemed to collect her thoughts. "This is when Stony decided he needed to protect his banks and his health. The plan was to keep Cindi and Holly close enough that he could keep tabs on them, but he was smart enough to realize they'd be the death of him if they continued to live under the same roof. He stuck Cindi in the nearest branch office and bought her a home, but kept it in his name. He kept her salary high enough that she wouldn't be tempted to strike out on her own but not so high that she wasn't dependent on him." Lou snapped her fingers. "Stony also installed an excellent security system that allowed him to monitor his daughter and granddaughter."

Fen turned onto the road leading to the university campus. "Are we getting close to the vacations you mentioned?"

"We're almost there," said Lou with a firm nod. "Between the cameras at the bank and the ones in Cindi's new home,

Stony could track his daughter day and night. Where he couldn't track Cindi was when she traveled or she and Holly went on vacations."

"I'm understanding," said Fen. "The only time Cindi could have any sort of social life was when she escaped the cameras."

Lou turned back to look out the windshield. "What I'm going to tell you now is what I learned from Cindi today. She started slow and didn't overplay her hand. For the first year in her new home she did nothing but go to work, go home, take care of Holly, and be a model employee for her father. Then she started going on overnight trips. They were always banking-related things that would increase her knowledge and skills. Longer conferences followed."

"Smart lady," said Fen.

"When Holly was fourteen they went on a short cruise out of Galveston. The next year, they went to Disney World. All the while, Cindi kept going to conferences."

Fen chuckled. "Where she met people and could let her hair down."

"Her biggest coup came when she took Holly to an all-inclusive resort last summer in the Dominican Republic. What she didn't tell Stony was, they each had their own rooms."

"And this week she has her own cabin while Holly stays in the dorm." Fen looked at the building the students were staying in. "Something tells me Cindi is taking advantage of the lack of cameras while she's here."

"You're the one who said she was panting the other night... and she doesn't like to go on hikes."

Fen parked and they met at the rear of his truck. "You're right. You can learn more than I thought by asking people about their vacations. We need to follow that thread and find out who might pay Cindi a visit at her cabin. It could be a nice, mostly respectable banker or it could be a killer."

"Or both," said Lou. "How are you planning on finding out?"

"Cindi will probably leave tonight or in the morning. A network of banks is now under her leadership, not to mention having to plan a funeral and grieve. I doubt she'll take much time cleaning the cabin she's staying in. That means tomorrow will be a good day for someone to visit the cabin and look around. Who knows, there might be more than one toothbrush in her bathroom."

"Let me guess," said Lou. "You want me to go."

"I'd do it, but tomorrow is my paint-and-think day."

Chapter Twenty-One

Sunday morning found Fen on the condo's balcony watching the world come to life as he sipped coffee. He'd already had his time with Sally, telling her he planned to paint most of the day. His goal was to get so lost in the painting that his mind would involuntarily meander into reviewing the clues of the two murders. Most of the time, all he had to show for his efforts was another work of art, but sometimes insights came to him as he painted. Either way it was time well spent. Amazingly, people wanted to buy them.

It took him by surprise when his phone alerted him to a text. He strode through the open patio door and saw Bailey's name.

Lousy night. Holly blames herself. Same for her mom.
Glad you took down the booth. Breakfast?

His plans for a quiet morning took a torpedo.

Lou says restaurant at Y.O. good. Meet in 20 minutes.

The response came back in a matter of seconds.

Make it 45. Need to shower.

An hour later, Bailey scurried into the restaurant and plopped down across from him. "Sorry I'm late. Thelma called and had to have all the details of Stony's death."

"Why am I not surprised? If parole officers kept tabs on their caseloads like Thelma does us, there'd be a lot less recidivism."

"It's my fault," said Bailey. "I introduced her to Google and social media. She's the most over-informed woman in Newman County."

Fen put down his coffee cup. "How long did you stay at the hospital?"

"Less than an hour. They put us in a little chapel instead of the emergency waiting area. A chaplain came and talked with us. Holly took it the hardest, but her mom was a close second. The manager of Mr. Gilmore's bank here in Kerrville came with his wife and helped Holly's mom get her head straight. He seemed to know a lot about Stony's medical problems."

"Lou knew about them too. It was only a matter of time. A lifetime of stress and bad genes killed Stony, not the argument at our booth."

"Speaking of the booth. Thanks for taking it down."

"All I did was supervise. Lou, Officer Craven, and a couple of city workers did the heavy lifting. You should thank them."

"I already thanked Brent. He's a nice guy."

Fen raised an eyebrow as a way of asking for more information.

"Lou called me last night and told me how the mayor and city council thought there was a curse on our booth."

"They didn't call it cursed, but now that you mention it..."

Bailey didn't respond to his attempt at humor but finished her thought, "She said you had the mayor stuttering and she thoroughly enjoyed it."

He ignored the compliment. "The mayor did us a favor. My heart wasn't into selling today and you wanted to be with Candice and Holly. We'll be back in business next weekend."

A server looked his way. He pantomimed for her to bring coffee for two.

Fen turned his head back to Bailey. "There's a nice buffet, or you can order off the menu. What will it be?"

She didn't hesitate. "Buffet. No one had an appetite last night so I waited until I got back to my room and ate a pack of those orange crackers with peanut butter between them."

"You must be starving."

"Nothing new about that. Let's eat."

Bailey returned to the table with food piled so high he wondered how she balanced it all. It was an unspoken agreement between them that talking ceased until Bailey had downed at least half her meal. This suited Fen as he'd settled for a bowl of cereal the preceding night and wondered if one helping of almost everything offered would be enough.

With a little more than half her breakfast devoured, Bailey raised her head, swallowed, and took a full drink of coffee. "That's better. I told you about my night. What did you do?"

He rested his fork on the side of his plate. "After Lou and I unloaded your paintings at the art studio, I took her back to her car. She was eager to write."

"About the murders?"

"She didn't say, but my guess is she wrote about them and the excitement at our tent."

Bailey sat up a little straighter. "I think Lou's up to something more than writing newspaper articles." She then filled her mouth with a large bite of biscuit with sausage gravy.

He picked up his fork and stabbed a bite of sausage but didn't pop it in his mouth. "What do you think she's writing?"

Bailey chewed and held up a finger for him to wait. As he continued with his meal she downed the bite and said, "I bet she's writing a book or perhaps a series of books about a former sheriff who goes around the state solving crimes."

Fen considered the possibility and bought time by chewing slowly and chasing the sausage with a drink of coffee. "Do you think these stories will be fiction or non-fiction?"

"I don't know. She probably doesn't know yet either. She's a cunning woman and will probably wait until she has more material before she decides."

With two murders to solve, Fen didn't want to clutter his mind with something that might never happen, so he moved on. "Are you going to paint today?"

She nodded. "What about you?"

He replied with a nod of his own. "There're only two things on my calendar today. First, I'm going to follow the advice I received from Officer Craven and add to a list I started last night."

"What list?"

"Jewell's autopsy shows the cause of death was asphyxiation. They found microscopic traces of metal on her throat. To be more specific, someone used a metal bar an inch and a half in diameter to crush her throat. Brent Craven suggested we make a master list of every type of pipe we can think of."

"How many did you come up with?"

"Only nine, but he's supposed to compile his own list."

Bailey looked up and to her left as she thought. "What about a shower-curtain rod?"

"That's ten and it might be the best one yet. Jewell was no stranger to hotel rooms."

Bailey nodded. "Wasn't she trying to hook up with

Candice's birth father again? I'd start with the curtain rod in his room."

"You're right." Fen pulled out his phone and scrolled until he found Ben Strange's number. The chief answered after the third ring.

"What's up, Fen?"

"This could be nothing, but I think it's worth checking out. We know a metal pipe was used to crush Jewell's throat. Right?"

"Correct."

"We also know that Jewell was plotting to lighten the wallets of all five of her ex-husbands again. Right?"

"That's what her daughter claims."

"I know this is a long shot, but what if she was putting her plan in motion and got friendly with ex number one and he saw through her plan?"

Ben mumbled something about his opinion of such a conniving woman but spoke clearly when he said, "It's possible."

Fen continued, "What if a shower rod or a metal closet rod is the murder weapon? It's possible there's still DNA or other evidence on it. Jewell, Jeremy Key, and Cliff Rouse were all staying at the Y.O."

Ben took up the story and ran with it. "I'll collect the rods myself and get them to the state lab today."

The call disconnected and Fen cast his gaze to Bailey, who looked too pleased with herself. "This is far from a done deal. Even if one ex-husband used a rod from the room, the suspects have had days to destroy the evidence. Why don't you start a list of pipes and rods too?"

"Me?"

"Yeah. You just thought of something that hadn't crossed my mind. It can't hurt to see what else you come up with."

Once again he changed the subject. "What can you tell me about what Holly and her mom's plans are for next week?"

"They left for home early this morning. Holly said she might come back tomorrow, but that depends on what her mom says."

He'd been associated with enough deaths to know the coming week would put a strain on Cindi. "Holly's mom is going to be super busy this week planning the funeral and transitioning to take her father's place at work. Holly will be left at home. I hope she can come back and paint."

"That's what Candice and I told her. Her mom seemed open to the idea." Bailey looked like she wanted to say something else.

"What is it?"

"It may be nothing, but Holly's mom kept getting phone calls last night."

"Any idea who?"

Bailey's long blond hair shook from side to side. "She seemed glad to receive the first call and went off by herself to talk. Then two calls came from someone she told not to call anymore."

"Any idea who?"

"I asked Holly. She said the first call was probably from a guy her mom's been interested in for quite a while. In fact, he was at the same resort they went to in the Dominican Republic last year. That's where Holly met a guy her age from Canada. He was shy and didn't kiss her until the night before she and her mom flew home. Nothing came of it after they left the resort. I guess her mom had better luck."

This confirmed his suspicions about Cindi breaking away from her father's domineering ways. Another question crossed his mind. "Do you think all three calls came from the same person?"

"Her reaction wasn't the same so I don't think so."

He looked down at his breakfast and pushed his plate away. The addition of information stilled his appetite and he longed to get in front of a canvas. It was time to take a step back from the investigation and put his mind in neutral. Answers to the tough questions seemed to come to him organically when he quit thinking so hard. Besides, Lou would search Cindi's cabin this morning and look for even more evidence of a man. Bailey and Brent Craven had their assignment of making a list of murder weapons, and Ben Strange was hot on the trail of evidence that could lead to an arrest and conviction. He'd learned a long time ago that solving crimes was a team effort. Best to take a step back and let others add their share to the case file.

Wanting to be alone he returned to the condo, set up an easel with a clean canvas on the balcony, and painted what was in front of him. The day passed with no thought of time until the light dimmed.

He cleaned his brushes and let his mind roam to the next days. He'd need to spend time with the students. The judging would take place Saturday morning, and he planned to drive home on Sunday night. He spoke to himself. "One week to solve two murders. I'd better turn my phone on and call Lou."

As soon as he brought his phone to life, it erupted with a missed-call message from Lou. He pushed the call-back function and waited for her to answer. He was on the verge of hanging up when she spoke. "It's about time. Next time you send me to break into a house, keep your phone on."

"It doesn't sound like you're calling from jail. That's good."

She let out a burst of disgust. "Of course I'm not in jail. Cindi must have been in such a hurry that she left the back door unlocked. I didn't even have to use my lock-picking tools."

"I don't know who's worse about wanting to pick locks—

you or Bailey." He walked to the refrigerator to get a bottle of water. "Did you find anything of interest?"

"A couple of things. The first was an unsigned note left on the front door. I took a photo of it and put it back where I found it. Hold on and I'll pull it up." The phone made some noises, and she spoke again.

Dear Cindi. Sorry about your dad. This changes every-thing. I'll be in touch.

"Nothing else?" asked Fen. "Was it handwritten?"

"No. It's been printed from a computer on standard paper."

"That doesn't help much. Anything else?"

"Yes, there's something else but you didn't give me time to tell you. Whoever wrote it signed it with the black and white yin yang symbol."

"That could mean many things. It suggests the duality of the universe. Good and evil. Even numbers and odd. Love and hate."

Lou interrupted, "It also represents male and female, and before you interrupt me again, the top portion was folded and torn off."

"Did it come in an envelope?"

"No. Just folded and stuck between the door and the frame."

Fen didn't speak for several seconds, which was long enough for Lou to ask, "Are you still there?"

"I'm thinking." He waited another few seconds before asking, "Did you find anything interesting inside the cabin?"

"Cindi didn't pack everything and take it home with her. She left enough clothes for a couple of days. Casual stuff like shorts, summer tops, and tennis shoes. The top drawer contained a baggy T-shirt and sleep shorts. I think she intends to come back next weekend."

"Perhaps she does. The doctor found no reason to order an autopsy on Stony so she can schedule the funeral for next week and be back for the contest on Saturday. I think Holly would like to finish her painting and compete."

"That's possible, especially since she and Candice are now best friends. Bailey told me Jewell's attorney is handling all the funeral arrangements and Candice is staying in the dorm until the day of her mom's funeral. I don't blame her for not going back to San Antonio and being alone in her mother's house."

Lou chuckled. "From the way Bailey talks about Mrs. Dillworth, she'll make sure Jewell's ex-husbands don't bother Candice."

"One last thing," said Lou. "Tucked underneath Cindi's modest sleepwear was lingerie. It's the type designed not to stay on very long."

"That answers another question I've been wondering about. Any other signs of a significant other?"

"One brown hair on the bathroom sink. Cindi's hair is long and blond."

"I hope you took it with you."

"It's in a plastic baggie. Do you want it?"

"Hang on to it for now. I'm betting now that Stony isn't around to browbeat Cindi, she'll tell us who it belongs to. Look for a man whose hair matches what you found when you go to Stony's funeral."

The call ended with the usual salutations. He kept the phone in his hand and told it to call Ben Strange.

"Please tell me you know who killed Jewell."

"Not yet, but we're making progress. Do you know the cabin that Cindi rented?"

"Sure do. We got her local address last night."

"There's a note stuck in her front door. It might be a good idea if you sent someone with gloves and an evidence bag to collect it."

"I guess it also needs to go to the state lab. Is this another long shot?"

"Not as long as the last one."

Chapter Twenty-Two

It was Monday morning and Fen couldn't still his mind. All seemed normal in the town when he passed through. City workers had put the park by the river back to rights and the students from the yoga class were dispersing after their early morning stretch. He traveled on, parked, and made his way to the university dining room. Droopy-eyed students dug sleep from their eyes and sipped either coffee or soft drinks.

A question made laps around his mind and he mumbled, "What have I missed?"

Things weren't clicking. Instead, he was experiencing a brain-itch. This wasn't a normal itch but one he couldn't put words to. It was like a mosquito had dined in the one place on his back he couldn't reach. Something in the investigation called out to him, a loose end that needed to be tied onto a longer string or snipped off and thrown away. He'd hoped the answer would come to him yesterday during his marathon painting session. No such luck.

His mental wanderings ended when Bailey's plate clattered

and she eased down in front of him. She asked, "Did you have a pleasant trip?"

"Huh?"

She picked up her fork. "You looked like you were a thousand miles from here."

"I have a brain-itch. I'm looking for an invisible stick to scratch it with."

A bite of bacon crunched when she bit into it. "Can't help you. All my brain cells are focused on Holly and her mom."

"What about Candice? How's she coping?"

"A little quieter than usual because of what happened to her mom, and she's worried about Holly and her mom." She swallowed a sip of coffee and spread red jelly on a piece of toast. "It seemed like everyone was a little off this morning. Roy lost his place during yoga and had us repeat the same position... twice. He had that thousand-yard stare you hear army guys talk about." She paused. "It was the same look you had when I sat down."

"Must be an epidemic." He took a sip of coffee. "Did Candice go to yoga?"

"We rode there together. She brought a can of Red Bull for each of us. If it wasn't for the jolt of caffeine, I'd have fallen asleep on my mat."

"Any word on the funeral for Candice's mom?"

The clatter of an empty plastic glass bouncing off the floor delayed her response. Bailey redirected her gaze. "Thursday afternoon. Her attorney took care of everything, including hiring off-duty police officers to make sure the five ex-husbands behave themselves."

"Smart move."

Bailey pushed her plate away and leaned forward. "What's bothering you this morning?"

Fen focused on the question, which delayed his response by

a few quiet seconds. "I'm missing something that's staring me in the face. Painting all day yesterday did no good. I had my morning talk with Sally and that didn't help either. I even took a walk along the river at dawn. It's like trying to pour something out of a bottle with the cork in it."

"That's a good visual. You should paint it and see what happens."

Instead of dismissing the suggestion he took it to heart. "You're on to something. I'll sketch it today." His gaze shifted to the students in the room. "In fact, that gives me an idea for all the students."

Bailey pulled her plate back and took up her fork. "Glad to help, but you have that mad scientist look in your eye. Have I created a monster?"

"He's a nice monster. You'll like him and he won't arrive until tomorrow evening."

"By the way," said Bailey as she spoke around a bite of bacon. "I called Holly last night. She's coming back tomorrow afternoon. They swamped her mom with funeral arrangements, plus taking over Stony's banks is more than a full-time job."

"Have they set a day and time for the funeral?"

"Thursday morning at ten o'clock."

Fen took a sip of coffee that had grown cold. "Two funerals in one day. I guess that means you, Holly, and Candice will go to both?"

"Unless you have something else for me to do."

He shook his head. "Lou will go, too. That's good. Both of you can make a list of people you recognize."

Bailey whispered. "Do you think the killer or killers might be there?"

"It wouldn't be the first time a murderer showed up at a funeral."

"Speaking of funerals." She stabbed a chunk of cottage-fried potato. "When is Rose Cunningham's?"

"Today. They didn't treat her autopsy with the same urgency as Jewell's."

Bailey let out a snort of disgust. "Even in death, Jewell gets preferential treatment."

He didn't respond to the statement other than to say, "Lou's going. You can stick around and paint."

"Good. I need to replenish my stock after Saturday's sales."

He stood and spoke as he stretched out a twinge of discomfort from having sat too long in the same position. "I'm going to the art studio and look at the submissions to the contest. I'm interested in seeing if anyone did any work over the weekend."

Bailey's mouth was at full capacity so she waved instead of answering.

The short walk to the art studio was enough to take the stiffness out of his knee. He reached for the doorknob as the door opened. Before him stood P.B., once again dressed in all black. They each tried to apologize for the awkward moment. Fen regained his bearings. "Are you coming or going?"

"Going. I needed more paint."

"Am I mistaken that I've seen nothing you've done since I looked at your sketch?"

"You're not imagining. I don't like to show my work until it's finished. That's why I paint in my room or sneak in here late at night."

She gave an open-mouthed yawn. "Sorry. It's past my bedtime."

Fen noticed her dark complexion poked through the white powder and her mascara needed refreshing. "Did you paint last night?"

"Every night. That's when I'm the most creative."

He tilted his head like a confused puppy. "Every night?"

"Between midnight and dawn are my favorite hours. I sleep during the day." She paused. "I went home Saturday evening. Dad showed me the work he bought from you. I wasn't expecting such depth of feeling. You really are a gifted artist."

"Thank you, but that's not my usual style. I wasn't sure it would ever sell."

"Most people don't embrace the duality of life. They want sunshine and rainbows without the mud and roiling black clouds of imminent destruction. It takes both."

"You're quite the philosopher, P.B. Do you want me to look at your work before you submit it?"

Instead of giving an off-the-cuff answer, she seemed to study the question. "Don't take this wrong but I'd prefer you didn't." She quickly added, "It's not that I don't respect your opinion. It's just that I studied the painting Dad bought for seven straight hours. I hope you don't mind but I'm incorporating some of your techniques, but not so many that they'll accuse me of plagiarism. I have to develop my style, but it will be an amalgamation of artists I admire."

Fen held up his hands. "I'm here to help, not to make clones."

"You've done your job and done it well."

P.B. drifted away. He wondered if she slept in a regular bed or a coffin. Saturday's competitions promised to be interesting... and hopefully without incident.

THAT EVENING he and Lou agreed their taste buds were calling out for fried catfish, so they met at THE LAKEHOUSE, a restaurant with a good rating and an exceptional view of the river. They scored a table next to a bank of windows, overlooking a stretch of water upstream from Fen's condo. Thanks to the first low-water dam, the river was wide and calm at this point. Lou ordered a beer on tap while Fen started with iced tea and an appetizer of fried mushrooms.

"Tell me about the funeral," said Fen. "See anyone you recognized?"

"Not a soul. Rose came from an enormous family so it was standing room only at the church. They played a slide show of her life that left everyone reaching for tissues. It's uncanny how much she resembled Jewell."

Fen considered the answer and moved on. "What about the graveside service? Anything unusual?"

"I stood on a rise away from the crowd. I couldn't hear the preacher but I've found that graveside services are all similar. Several people left a little early, most didn't come because of the heat." She issued a crooked smile. "After an hour and a half church service, I think most people needed to give their ears a break."

The drinks arrived and the server announced, "Your appetizer will be ready any minute. Are you ready to order your meals?"

"Not yet," said Fen. "We're expecting one more to join us."

The young man responded with a nod, took a step back, and disappeared.

Fen took his phone from his pocket and placed it on the table. "Thanks for the photos and videos. I'll give them a thorough look tonight when I get back to the condo."

Lou leaned forward and lowered her voice. "It took a while, and I felt like a car thief. Are you sure you needed the license plate of every car in the parking lot?"

He brought his gaze back to her. "Did anyone confront you?"

"Not with words, but it's a good thing I'm used to people trying to make me feel uncomfortable. The looks I received could turn steam into snow." Lou tilted her head. "Why did you have me get images of the license plates?"

"Another long shot. I want you to do the same thing at the two funerals on Thursday."

"Why?"

He put his elbows on the table. "What did Rose Cunningham have in common with Jewell?"

"Nothing I know of, other than being drop-dead beautiful."

"Right. There's nothing we can find that linked them other than they could be mistaken for each other."

Lou's eyebrows went up. "Are you still thinking Rose was mistaken for Jewell?"

"I haven't ruled it out."

He took a sip of his tea and realized it was unsweetened. Reaching for sugar packets, he tore three open, dumped them into his glass, and stirred as he continued. "Let's pretend the killer made a mistake and killed the wrong woman. Let's also pretend he's a sociopath who gets his jollies from other people's misery. Those sickos go to the funerals of their victims."

Lou interjected, "Like some arsonists who start a fire, leave the scene, then come back and watch the firefighters put out what they started."

"Exactly."

"That means you expect to find the killer at Jewell's funeral, and you'll identify him by tracing his license plate."

Fen glanced toward the river. "There's only a few dozen ways I could be wrong about it, but I'm willing to try anything."

A man's voice came from over his shoulder. "Sorry I'm late. The mayor insisted on a personal update of the cases."

Fen motioned for Chief Strange to take the empty chair facing the window. He declined and came around the table to put the river at his back. "I've been a cop long enough to know it's best to keep your back to a wall." He glanced at the river. "Or in this case, to keep the distracting view behind me."

Lou shook her head. "The funniest thing to watch is when a group of cops tries to beat each other to seats where they can watch the room."

The fried mushrooms arrived and the server took another order for iced tea.

Fen faced the chief and asked, "Did you receive the reports from the state crime lab?"

"Yep, and we're no closer to solving either case. No DNA, makeup, or anything on the rods. Ray-Ray has small hands that don't fit the bruising patterns on Rose's throat. The DA's keeping a lid on the results but that eliminates our one and only suspect in Rose Cunningham's murder. It's just a matter of time before we have to release him."

"What about the letter in the door of Cindi's cabin?"

"They're still processing it but I'm not holding out much hope for that either."

Ben's iced tea arrived and he took a long drink before setting the glass on the table. "Anything new for me from either of you?"

Fen pointed across the table. "Lou went to Rose Cunningham's funeral today. I'll let her tell you about it."

She gave him the abridged version.

Fen took up where Lou left off. "She didn't tell you this part. I asked Lou to walk the parking lot and take photos of all the license plates. She'll do the same on Thursday at Stony and Jewell's funerals." He then explained why.

Ben didn't look or sound convinced. "I guess if you keep taking long shots, you'll eventually hit something. I'm under pressure to get overtime off the books and can't send anyone to help you."

"It's a one-woman job," said Fen.

Lou swallowed a bite of fried mushroom. "You'd think I'd tire of chasing false leads, but some of my biggest stories came about when I was sure I was wasting my time following a hunch."

Ben asked, "Is this hunch of yours saying Rose wasn't the intended victim?"

She pointed at Fen. "You can blame former sheriff Maguire for that brainstorm. Every now and then he gets lucky and guesses right."

The server returned and took orders of fried catfish all around with Ben having his inside catfish tacos.

Fen snapped his finger. "I just remembered something. Brent Craven sent me a list of the pipes that might have been used to crush Jewell's throat."

"He did?" said Ben.

"Sent it today, bright and early."

"That must have been before he tore some muscles. He was lifting weights in his garage when one of those toothpick arms gave out." Ben's eyes shifted to watch someone come into the room. "I didn't know you asked him to make a list. Is that where you got the idea for the shower rods?"

"Indirectly. Officer Craven came up with the idea. I added to the list and Bailey suggested we look at the shower and curtain rods since the victim and suspects were all staying at the Y.O. Resort."

"It's still a good idea to make a list," said Lou.

Ben cast his gaze toward Fen and lowered his voice. "I don't want to spoil the evening, but the mayor told me the city council isn't happy with the progress we're making. There's a regular monthly meeting scheduled for next Wednesday night, and I'm to give an update."

"That doesn't sound too bad," said Lou.

"There's also time set aside for them to meet in a closed session to discuss a personnel issue."

Fen puffed out his cheeks. "I'm leaving town as soon as I can get packed Sunday afternoon. That means we don't have much time to find our killer."

"Deadlines," said Lou with exasperation seasoning the word. "Why is my life controlled by deadlines?"

"I can't answer that," said Ben, "but I feel like I'm a turkey, it's the week before Thanksgiving, and the farmer is looking for his ax."

"You have nothing to worry about," said Fen. After a dramatic pause, he continued, "At least not yet. If you see sparks flying after that farmer finds his ax, start running."

Chapter Twenty-Three

Wednesday morning found Fen back at the university with students wearing paint-stained jeans and T-shirts, ready to get started on yet another day of creating works to submit to the judges. He knew from experience that as the deadline for a contest loomed, the stress of finishing would increase. He stood before the noisy group, stuck his thumb and forefinger in his mouth, and let out a shriek of a whistle. All conversations ceased and he had their undivided attention.

Bailey came in late, leading a bleary-eyed P.B. She wore her standard black but had not taken the time to put on the white foundation or thick makeup that made her look like she was auditioning for a part in a black and white horror movie.

"Listen up," he said in his cop's voice. "There's more to being an artist than what you've experienced since you came here. Life will throw you curveballs and you have to learn what it means to be flexible and work under stress. I've tried to impress upon you how important time management is. Most of you paid attention and set daily goals so you'll finish in time to present a finished work that represents the best you can do. Some of you ignored the advice. It's time you learned a lesson that you'll never forget."

The student's blank stares told him they weren't tracking what he was saying so he continued, "We're going on a field trip today to the prayer and sculpture garden on the north side of town. Your assignment for the morning is to find a sculpture that speaks to you and complete a detailed sketch. No private cars today. Everyone is to get on the bus. This afternoon and evening you're to complete an acrylic painting of the sculpture you chose."

A voice came from the front row. "That's not fair. You're changing the rules."

"Life isn't fair," he said in a stern voice.

A second voice said, "I set my painting schedule to finish on Friday morning. Now I won't have time."

More voices joined in, complaining about the changes.

"Quiet!" he shouted as he took a step forward. "Is it fair that someone murdered Candice's mother, or that Holly's grandfather died on Saturday? Candice will miss an entire day of painting and Holly has already missed two days and she'll miss another tomorrow. They won't be joining us today, so they can stay here and try to catch up. If anyone thinks that isn't *fair*, talk to me about it tomorrow. I don't want to hear it today."

Not a peep came from anyone in the room. He softened his voice. "Every student who completes today's assignment will receive one hundred dollars. The best sketch will receive two hundred dollars, as will the best painting." He pointed. "The bus is waiting. Grab your sketch pads and pencils."

P.B. took her time gathering her supplies. He made his way to her and said, "I know you stayed up all night. I'm not expecting anything great out of you and if you need to stay on the bus and sleep, that's fine with me."

She tilted her head. "How many times did you stay up all night when you were sheriff, only to put in another full day?"

"Plenty."

"Don't worry about me. I budgeted for two extra days on my schedule. Besides, I'm looking for one more element to add to my painting. I think it has something to do with despair and hope. The prayer and sculpture garden might be the place to find it."

Fen was thinking about how he'd misjudged P.B. when Bailey sidled up beside him. "I made the same mistake about her. She's the real deal."

"One of a kind. She'll go far."

They cleared the building and approached the bus. "What time did Holly get in last night?"

"Just before dark. Holly said her mom's super busy."

"Any sign of a man in her life?"

"She didn't come out and say it but I think there is."

"You should know for sure at the funeral. Pay attention to how the men hug and shake hands with her. Also, look for anyone she keeps looking at."

Bailey stopped before she made it to the bus and threw a thumb over her shoulder. "You're doing a good job with the students. They needed a good kick in the rear."

"There's always a tendency to slack off near the end. That's when students get in trouble."

"Is that the voice of experience?"

He responded with a guilty smile. "Let's get on the bus while I still have my bluff in on them."

The morning traffic was light and they made it to the north side of town without incident. In fact, the students seemed to have forgotten about their cries for fairness and were rising to the challenge. The promise of getting paid for their labor worked like carrots on strings in front of a herd of mules. Plans floated back and forth for how they'd spend their newfound wealth.

The bus groaned its way up a steep, windy road and settled in a parking lot near the top of a hill with a commanding view of the town of Kerrville and Interstate 10, a concrete and asphalt artery that connects Southern California with Florida. The students piled out of the bus and assembled without being told to do so. It reminded him of soldiers waiting for their commanding officer to issue orders.

He pointed. "This is a special place with many sculptures. Don't rush your decision of which one you want to sketch. I suggest you walk and work alone but it's your decision. We'll meet back here at eleven-forty-five."

Bailey walked with him until they reached the summit. She turned and stared at the river valley below. "Wow," she whispered. She held out her right hand and allowed it to travel from west to east. "I'm all in for this view. I'm going to paint it twice. Once the way it looked two hundred years ago and another the way it looks today."

"That's ambitious."

"True, but I'm thinking about how it will sell. I can sell individual prints or a set."

"Good thinking. You're getting better at looking at settings from both an artistic and commercial perspective. Be sure you take photos. Panoramic scenes are quite the challenge."

He lost Bailey to her passion for art. A path to the left led him away from the summit. On his right and left were white stones, some larger than others. Upon closer inspection, the stones had prayers written on them. Instead of flowers in the prayer garden, there were literal prayer stones. He found a bin of pure white rocks and picked out a couple. He found a bench with shade, closed his eyes, and allowed the sense of peace to envelope him. His mind strayed to the clues of the killings. He focused on his breathing and heart rate until both were reduced to the point he sensed he might fall asleep. He likened this state of being to a car in neutral on a flat surface. If people walked past him he didn't hear them. If a breeze kicked up he didn't feel it.

He couldn't say how long he stayed on the bench. All he knew was that he didn't want to leave it. In this vacuum all he could do was listen. It was sacrilege to do anything else.

What happened next put an icy shiver down his spine. A silent voice that sounded like his late wife said, "Tie up the loose end."

His eyes flew open. He was back in the prayer garden with two white stones on the bench beside him. He took a Sharpie out of his shirt pocket and wrote two prayers of thanksgiving. One was to Sally for the years she endured being married to a state trooper and a sheriff. The second went to the Lord for guiding his steps. The prayer rocks joined the others in the bed along the path. He looked at the time on his phone. He'd been on the bench for over two hours.

As he walked on and examined the sculptures it occurred to him that Sally hadn't told him what the loose end was. It didn't matter. It was his job to find it, and he knew he would. Confidence rose in him with every step, like a fast-rising river.

By eleven thirty he'd checked on every student and their sketches. He looked to the horizon as black clouds embedded with streaks of light raced toward them from the west. The door to the bus closed at eleven forty-five. Lightning struck so close there was only a split second between the flash and the explosion of thunder. Students screamed. By the time they made it down the hill, rain pelted them so hard the driver dared not exceed fifteen miles an hour on the way back to the university.

Lunch was noisy and short. The students were eager to get

to work earning their hundred dollars. Fen had a desire to get home and dive into the folder that he believed held the solution to the murders.

Mrs. Dillworth had other ideas. She stood before him with her chin elevated and posture that made her look like the dry cleaners had returned her after applying heavy starch and a hot iron. "Mr. Maguire, we have a problem."

"Oh? And what would that be?"

"Actually, there are several problems." She looked around. "I prefer not to discuss them with children present."

His initial reaction was to challenge her on the status of the young men and women. In his mind they'd stopped being children many years prior. He tamped down the urge to correct her perhaps because of the residual effects of the prayer garden. Instead he asked, "Where and when would you like to meet?"

"Follow me to the dorm. Business is to be conducted in the proper setting, not where anyone can hear."

He stood. "Lead on."

Once in the dorm she entered an office and took the place of power in a wooden chair behind a plain desk. The office had all the charm of a prison cell with no pictures on the walls, no framed photos of family on the desk, and no mementos on the windowsill. She did, however, have a file folder sitting directly in front of her and an old-school phone off to one side. Her head bobbed in the general direction of the chair on his side of the desk. Then came a one-word command. "Sit."

"No thanks," he said as he went to the window and looked out. "Look at that rain. I bet three inches have already come down. If this keeps up, there'll be flash floods."

Her response was a terse, "I wanted to talk to you about your behavior since you've been here, not receive a weather report. I hope I won't have to file a formal complaint."

He kept looking out the window. "A formal complaint? This must be serious."

"You've fostered an atmosphere that's led some of the students to break university policy."

"What policy would that be?" When he turned around, she was pulling a clear plastic bag with six empty cans of beer from the desk. She pointed. "I found these in the communal trash can on the girl's wing." She then pulled out a second clear bag containing cigarette butts. "And these were in the boy's wing. I find new ones every day."

Fen picked up the bag containing the collection of cans. "I don't drink this brand. As for the cigarettes, I don't smoke."

She let out a huff. "I have it on good authority that you knew about these infractions and didn't notify me."

"Isn't overseeing the welfare of the students in the dorm your responsibility?"

She ignored the question. "You've been negligent in your duties of instructing the students. You haven't led them in any classroom instruction, and I know for certain that one girl sleeps all day, wears outlandish clothes, and sometimes paints in the art studio at night."

Fen nodded that he understood the complaint. "What else?"

"Your relationship with that Bailey Madison girl. Is it true that she lives with you and she's already completed a semester of college?" A look of smug satisfaction came with the veiled accusations. She added. "I'm sure the president and chancellors will be interested to know you live with a minor and got her a special dispensation to compete in the summer program and contest."

Instead of erupting Fen sat on the corner of her desk. He pulled out his phone and placed it in front of her. "If you want to call the university president and make a fool out of yourself, be my guest." He lowered his voice to a whisper. "Before you do, you need to know what will happen."

She swallowed.

"My responsibility for the art students is to supervise their development as artists. That's it, and that's what I've done. I have my own reasons for teaching the way I do that I'll be glad to discuss with the president. You've never talked to me before holding this inquisition. Why is that?"

"I still say you're a bad influence on the children."

He brushed the comment aside. "Do you really think the president will blame me for something that's in your job description?"

After only a quick breath, he continued, "As for my relationship with Bailey, she lives above my garage in a separate apartment. She has her own studio and my housekeeper is her chaperone. She's a pupil of mine and is not taking part in the contest."

"Then she shouldn't be with the other students."

Fen ran a hand down his cheek. "It seems you've made some false assumptions, Mrs. Dillworth."

"I think not. I've supervised this dorm for twenty-eight years and I can tell the difference between students who belong here and those who won't conform to rules and our high standards."

Fen gave her a toothy smile. "Whose standards and rules are you referring to? The university's or the ones you invent for two weeks every summer?"

"The university trusts me to run a tight ship."

He'd grown weary of the back and forth and lifted the receiver to the phone on her desk and handed it to her. "Make your call. You might as well call the chief of police and the mayor while you're at it. They've invited me to help investigate the recent murders. The president is fully aware of this and that Bailey is my assistant. She's already helped me solve two murders and is helping me again. As for the activities of the other students, I'll talk to the students if you can prove who drank the beer, smoked the cigarettes in the dorm, or violated any written rule. P.B. Brown's sleeping and painting habits fall under my jurisdiction. She has my permission to paint late at night. She's not breaking any rules or disturbing anyone but you. As for her clothing, it's more discreet than what you're wearing."

He placed the receiver on the desk and leaned over. In a whisper, he asked, "Do you really want to interfere in murder investigations? If so, you could be subject to arrest."

He turned on his heel and left the confines of the office.

On the way to the art studio he almost felt sorry for Mrs. Dillworth until he remembered that bullies came in all shapes, sizes, and ages. He checked in with Bailey, put her in charge of the studio, and traveled back to the condo to look for the loose end he'd missed in the file folder.

Rain streaked his patio window and what had been a calm lake turned into a fast-moving highway for sticks, logs, and unnamed flotsam. He could only imagine how the river looked below the second dam. After heating the morning's leftover coffee in the microwave, he focused on the thick files of information. The thin one had Rose Cunningham's name on it. Jewell's file bulged with pages. Something told him he'd find his answer in the thick file.

He finished the second reading of the file when a ray of light pierced the dark clouds. He went back to the beginning and started over. After two more times through the file, he glanced at the clock and realized it was almost Thursday morning. His eyes traveled over a handwritten note he'd made based on a conversation with Stony. The words all but jumped off the page. Stony had followed Holly's biological father, Roger Slade, for five years after he paid him off and the young man moved to California.

"There's the loose end," said Fen. He looked up. "Thanks, Sally."

Chapter Twenty-Four

Eight in the morning seemed like a decent enough time to begin phone calls. The first, and most important one, went to Chuck and Candy Forsythe at their law office back in Newman County.

Chuck answered with a question. "How high's the water? I hear it's been a little damp in Kerrville."

Fen was staring out the patio door. "It's almost to the top of the bank and rising. It must be rolling something fierce below the second dam."

Candy spoke up. "How're the investigations?"

"I'm on the track of something but I need help. It's a loose end that eluded me until last night."

"Give us the details."

He explained how Stony had exiled Holly's birth father to California and tracked him for five years before deciding Roger Slade had no interest in Cindi or the child.

Chuck asked, "Why can't Lou track him for you? She's the queen of snooping."

"Lou's attending two funerals today." He then explained

how she was looking for someone attending both funerals by taking photos of license plates.

"This sounds like bean soup with no beans... awful thin," said Chuck.

"I'm not so sure," said Candy. "What's your gut telling you, Fen?"

He wouldn't admit this to anyone but the few people he trusted with his life. "I can't explain it, but I think Sally's helping me with this one."

Candy didn't hesitate. "I'll do what I can and get back to you."

Once again Fen had questions about how Chuck and Candy, a small-town lawyer and his wife, had access to information that rivaled the FBI and CIA combined. He'd asked a long time ago and Chuck told him the less he knew, the better. Fen accepted this and found contentment in knowing people were watching out for him, albeit from a distance.

With the first call out of the way, he told his phone to call Bailey. He heard what sounded like traffic noise in the background. "Have you left yet?"

"Candice is filling up her car. I'm in the truck stop picking up coffee and pastries. We skipped breakfast in the cafeteria."

"You'll get to San Antonio in plenty of time."

"Candice's attorney needs to talk to her before the funeral. It seems big money comes with enormous responsibilities and headaches."

"Don't forget the privilege of paying higher taxes, too." He looked at the coffeepot and decided against another cup. "Make yourself available to come over for pizza tonight. You can give us a report of how Jewell's ex-husbands acted. Also, keep your eyes open this afternoon for anyone who looks interested in Holly's mom."

Bailey chuckled. "I can tell by your voice you're onto something... or someone."

"Lou and the chief of police might be here, too. Call me when you get back to town and I'll let you know what time to come."

"Holly and Candice are planning on painting all night, making up for today. Pizza with you is better than supper with Mrs. Dillworth staring at me."

Fen rubbed his neck. "Did she say anything to you last night?"

"It's strange. She normally roams the halls looking for something to gripe about and doing bed checks at ten thirty. She was nowhere to be seen and a lot of the students worked late into the night."

He was glad Bailey couldn't see his mischievous smile. "I need to call Lou. See you tonight."

Lou answered in a chipper voice. "Good morning. You caught me on my way to breakfast."

"You sound well rested."

"Put me in a room with a window so I can look at a thunderstorm and I can pump out thousands of good words. I hit flow state yesterday afternoon and did two days' worth of writing in one."

"I hope you didn't stay up too late. You have a big assignment today."

"I was hoping you changed your mind about that. Are you sure you want me to film the license plate on every car at both funerals and graveside services?"

He nodded, even though she couldn't see him. "Positive. I called Chuck and Candy this morning. To make a long story short, I have a new suspect. You're busy today so Candy's trying to track him down."

"Who is it?"

"If I tell you, you'll start an online search for him and conveniently forget about filming the license plates."

He expected an explosion. She didn't disappoint. He held his phone out as she let him verbally have both barrels. She ended with, "Why do you take such delight in dangling stories in front of me and then jerking them away?"

"It's fun to make your teeth itch." He ended the conversation with, "Pizza at the condo tonight. Bailey, Chief Strange, you, and me. I still need to confirm that Ben can make it. Even if he can't, the three of us are going to meet."

"You sound like you're close to solving the murders."

"I'll let you know tonight."

The last call went to Ben Strange.

"The mayor expects me at nine o'clock for a morning briefing."

Fen cut the conversation short. "Tell the mayor you're making substantial progress and expect a breakthrough any day. Can you come to my condo tonight? Free food and drinks."

"Best offer I'm likely to get all day. What time?"

"Does seven work for you?"

"I'll make it work."

The call came to an abrupt end, and it was time to get to the university and quell deadline jitters among the students. Their paintings would go to the judges on Friday afternoon. Not much time remained.

THE DAY PASSED with Fen's time split between calming the nerves of anxious students and mentally reviewing the details of the case and searching for other loose ends. They still hadn't identified what the murder weapon might be. It seemed important, but by the afternoon he'd concluded that it wasn't on the master list of types of pipes. Frustration set in. He'd never admit it to Lou, but he sensed his teeth itching.

His time with the students ended at six o'clock. Several procrastinators waited until the last full day of painting to ask him for advice. This was typical for students used to cramming for exams and their work showed their lack of commitment. He learned a long time ago that failure was a better teacher than scolding. They'd learn on Saturday that their works wouldn't earn even an honorable mention.

With a day filled with conversations emphasizing the importance of detail and style behind him, he arrived at the condo and placed an order for pizza. What he didn't expect was a call from Thelma as soon as he slipped his phone back into the pocket of his shirt. She started the conversation with a question. "Are you and Bailey all right?"

He scratched the back of his head. "Sure. Why wouldn't we be?"

"The news reports are saying the Guadalupe is killing people. There's been four people drowned and property damage in the millions."

Once again Thelma was following her dual proclivity to gather information and worry. She prided herself on being the go-to person who had inside information on people and current events. She'd soon make the rounds with texts and phone calls to deliver the latest news related to the great flood.

He continued the conversation with, "I haven't kept up with the news twenty-four hours a day, but I believe the river is supposed to crest today. It rained as hard as I've ever seen it yesterday, but I've only heard of a couple of really low-lying streets flooding."

This was enough detail to give her something to embellish and share with her tribe of information gatherers.

"Are you sure Bailey's high and dry?"

"I spoke with her this afternoon. She's fine. In fact, she and Lou are coming over in a few minutes for pizza."

"I hope you ordered salads to go with that. I don't want to have to lecture you again about getting constipated because you don't eat like you know you should."

Fen rolled his eyes. "I ordered everyone a salad."

"Are you still coming home Sunday night?"

"We might come home a day early. The river's covering the park where the vendors set up tents. I haven't heard if there's an alternate location on the high side of the river."

"I'll rest a lot better when I know you're away from that river. You let me know so I can stop worrying."

It wasn't more than fifteen minutes after the call that Bailey arrived. The first words out of her mouth were, "What's this about us going home a day early? I need to sell some more paintings."

He let out a low chuckle. "Thelma must have called you the second our call ended. I told her it was a possibility because the river is covering the park where we set up this past weekend."

Bailey settled on the couch. "I should've known you're not up to date on the latest. The city is blocking off the main street downtown and diverting traffic. Brent Craven got us a prime location for our booth in front of the cultural arts center."

"Perfect. With any luck, we'll wrap up the cases and pad our bank accounts too."

She looked at him with raised eyebrows. "I didn't realize you're that close to solving both murders."

"Only if everything falls into place and there are no surprises."

He'd settled into the recliner when another knock sounded on the door. Bailey sprang to her feet. "I'll get it."

"It's Lou, Chief Strange, or the pizza delivery."

Chapter Twenty-Five

B en Strange, Lou, and a pizza delivery driver wearing a red baseball cap over lavender-colored hair arrived within three minutes of each other. Fen dutifully ate his salad first, as did Bailey. Neither wanted to receive another lecture from Thelma on the benefits of roughage. Everyone engaged in small talk, mainly about the river and downstream damage. Once again, the two dams had spared the town and most likely saved lives.

Bailey had a teenager's appetite, so Fen called on Lou after she'd eaten most of her salad and two slices of pizza. She looked at Bailey and said, "I don't know about yours, but my day was a lot of work for nothing. Unless I missed something, no one at Jewell's funeral went to Stony's except you, Candice, and Holly." She paused. "Not unless they went in different vehicles."

"I hadn't thought of that," said Fen. "But it's not likely."

Bailey broke in. "Did you see the five ex-husbands squabbling over who should sit in the front row of the funeral home?"

Lou might as well have spit out the answer. "Someone told

me I needed to stay in the parking lot and take pictures of a bunch of stupid license plates. I could have worked the actions of the exes into a story. As it is, I'll need Bailey's account to go with the fight at Jewell's graveside service."

Ben sat up straight. "The exes fought at the burial?"

Lou gave a firm nod. "Three of them did, but not until the service was over." She added, "They at least had the decency not to start swinging until they were on the way to their cars. The only reason I got footage of it was because I was walking back from filming the last of the license plates."

Fen broke in. "Did any cars stand out to you?"

"The number of vanity license plates surprised me. There were also a few from out of state."

Fen considered the last statement and said, "With so many people moving into Texas these days, that's not surprising. Also, it's not uncommon for people to put off registering their cars for months."

He shifted his gaze to Bailey. "Did anything else catch your eye at Jewell's funeral?"

"Yeah. Those ex-husbands are crazy. It took me, Holly, two men from the funeral home, and threats from Candice's attorney to keep them away from Candice. It was like they were trying to save a part of Jewell." Her head tilted as she asked, "Is it love or money that makes people lose their marbles?"

"Either, and sometimes both," said Lou. "I can't think how much it would have pleased Jewell to know men were still nuts about her even after she died."

Fen tried to get back to business. His gaze fixed on Bailey. "Tell us about Stony's funeral."

"None of the drama. Very professional and reverent."

"Did anyone sit with Holly's mom beside Holly?"

"Not at the church, but there was a nice-looking man her

age that gave her an extra-long hug after the graveside service. They looked like they belonged together, if you know what I mean. Holly said he's been coming around for a long time, pretending he needs to talk to her about banking stuff. His name is Karl Mahew. He's the one who was at the all-inclusive resort when Holly and her mom were there."

Lou said, "That's one mystery solved. I bet they'll be together for the awards ceremony on Saturday. No need to keep secrets with Stony below ground."

Ben looked at Fen and asked, "Do you want me to run him through the database?"

"Might as well, even though I seriously doubt anything will show up. I bet he's a nice guy with an abundance of patience."

The musical notes from Fen's phone caused him to jerk it out of the pocket of his shirt. He rose after checking the caller ID and announced. "I have to take this in private. Finish your meal and we'll go over everything in a few minutes."

He answered as he headed for the privacy of the master bedroom. "Hang on a minute, I'm going somewhere private." The bathroom door closed behind him. "Ok, Candy. No one can hear us. What did you find out?"

"Not as much as I hoped for. It seems Holly's birth father got married five years after he arrived in California."

Fen broke in. "That explains why Stony quit keeping tabs on him. What else?"

"Perhaps he should have kept up the surveillance. The marriage only lasted six months before he put her in the hospital and received a six-year sentence."

"No probation?"

"He almost killed her; and like Cindi, his wife came from a family with money."

"Now it makes sense."

Candy continued. "According to prison records and an

assistant warden that remembered him, Roger Slade went through a tough time the first couple of years he was locked up. He got tired of being the victim and rebuilt himself physically. He got in with a small group of musclebound inmates who protected each other."

"Was it a recognized gang?"

"No. There were never over five at a time and they kept a low profile. It seems their only goal was self-preservation and to get out as soon as possible."

"Interesting," said Fen.

"There's more. After release, Roger still had a couple of years to do on parole. No more arrests, even though they could have sent him back for association with known felons... his buddies from prison. His parole officer thinks they joined forces with a shady lawyer. She didn't know what things he got into, but he received a regular paycheck working as a consultant."

"That could mean anything."

The sound of a page turning came through the phone. Candy moved on. "About nine months ago, Roger Slade ceased to exist. The last thing I found on him is that he closed a series of bank accounts."

"How much did he take out?"

"A little over three hundred thousand dollars from a dozen different banks. All in cash."

Fen let out a whistle. "That's a good nest egg. What do you and Chuck think happened to him?"

"Chuck said that was for you to figure out. I think that if he's still alive, he has a lot more than three hundred grand and could be anywhere in the world."

His mind was turning like a lab mouse on a metal wheel. He thanked Candy and rejoined the gathering as they were putting paper plates in the trash. For the next few hours, they went through every scrap of information and gave theories about the importance of each one. He'd hoped to tie up the loose end of where Holly's father was. That hadn't panned out the way he'd hoped.

Although he still didn't have enough evidence to prove it, Fen maintained his theory that Rose Cunningham's homicide resulted from a simple case of mistaken identity. Jewell's murder, however, was deliberate and savage. For someone to press down hard on her throat with a metal bar meant they were behind her, or looking into her eyes as life left her.

Lou and the chief weren't as sure about Fen's single killer theory. Bailey took Fen's side of the debate but couldn't give a good reason why.

The next loose end was the note found in the door of Cindi's cabin. Anyone could have written it, but most likely it came from Karl Mahew, Cindi's love interest. They decided the quickest way was to ask Mr. Mahew and go from there.

Finally there was the elephant in the room—motive. Who had reason enough to kill Jewell? Of all the missing puzzle pieces, this one brought the most debate. From what everyone had been told, to know Jewell was both to love her and hate her. Names flew like a dozen balloons filled to the max with air and released without tying them off. Soon enough all the guesses lay on the living room floor.

Instead of prolonging everyone's misery, Fen called an end to the meeting around eleven. "Let's all sleep on it. Tomorrow's Friday and we still have a few days before Bailey, Lou, and I leave town."

Ben Strange stood. "I might be right behind you driving a U-Haul."

Bailey put her hand on the chief's shoulder. "A lot can happen in three days with Fen. I wouldn't pack yet."

Chapter Twenty-Six

B lue light from the digital alarm clock on the bedside table cast a spectral hue across the otherwise dark bedroom. Fen cracked open an eye and read 5:03 a.m. He did the math and realized he'd slept a mere two hours and twelve minutes. The feather pillows seemed to pull him downward, coaxing him to roll over and wait at least another hour to push the sheet and duvet back. His mind, however, refused to comply. He turned over and his hand slapped the file folder he'd brought to bed. He knew it was his imagination but he could almost hear the contents of the file tell him to get up.

He turned on the light. During the night, he must have thrashed. Papers lay strewn across the duvet on the king-size bed. "If you have something to say, say it. I've lost way too much sleep during the last two weeks."

The room remained silent.

He rose, staggered to the bathroom, turned on the shower, and adjusted it to a comfortable setting. What happened next caused him to stop washing his hair in mid-lather. With eyes closed, he had the sensation that all the clues were coming together to form a mosaic made of brightly colored pieces of tile.

He hurried to remove the shampoo as another sensation hit him like someone had replaced the water coming from the shower head with water taken from under the ice of a frozen lake. Danger. He sensed it with such intensity that goose bumps rose on his skin.

He may or may not have gotten all the soap off but that didn't matter. The killer was going to strike again if he didn't do something and do it quick. Wrapping a towel around his waist, he left a trail of water from the bathroom to the dresser where he'd left his cell phone charging. He reached for it but didn't know who to call first. Closing his eyes, he spoke to himself. "You know what to do. Make a plan and work it. Think. Step number one is to call Cindi."

He had to rummage through the file to find her number. After punching in the digits, he waited until it rang twelve times before giving up. Not good. Time to think out loud again.

"Her cabin is outside the city limits. That's the sheriff's jurisdiction. If I call them to do a wellness check, it will take me too long to convince them I'm not a crackpot. That's a low-priority call, and it might be an hour or more before a deputy would get there."

He brought his phone to life again and told it to call Lou. Six rings then one more before a voice that sounded like a poorly tuned cello finally said, "I'm not taking calls until after nine o'clock."

"Put your feet on the floor and listen."

A groan, the faint sound of covers rustling, and a salty expletive came through his phone's speaker. "This is going to cost you."

"Listen carefully. I don't have time to explain. Get to Cindi's cabin as quick as you can."

"Did you try calling her?"

"I let it ring twelve times." He paused, but only to take a breath. "She'll be the next victim if we don't get moving. Take your lock-picking tools and call me ASAP."

Lou went into full reporter mode. "Are you sure? What's the motive? Who's the killer?"

He'd already mentally moved on to his next call. Instead of responding, he pushed the end call icon on the face of his phone. Lou would cuss him all the way to Cindi's cabin but he'd worry about that later.

Still wearing only a towel, he instructed his phone to call Bailey. She answered on the fourth ring and her voice didn't have near the gravelly sound to it that Lou's did. "It's early. What's the matter?"

"Everything is busting loose. Get down to Holly's room and make sure she's there."

"If I bang on her door, I'll wake up half the girls in the dorm."

"Then call her first. If she doesn't answer, start banging. I don't care if you wake up half the town. We have to find her and her mom."

One thing Fen appreciated about Bailey was that she had enough street smarts about her to discern drama from real trouble. Her quick response proved it. "I'm putting you on hold."

He waited for less than a minute. It felt like an hour.

"She's not answering. I'm already at her door."

Loud, repeated banging came. Then Bailey hollered Holly's name. "She's not answering. Let me try her door... it's unlocked... she's not here."

"I was afraid of that. Where could she have gone?"

"Candice is here. I'll ask her."

"Candice, wake up. Something important is going on. Do you know where Holly is?"

He heard a groggy voice say, "She went to her mom's cabin to spend the night."

Bailey's voice came back strong. "Did you hear that?"

"I heard, but her mom isn't answering her phone and now neither is Holly." He ran a hand through wet hair. "Any ideas where they might have gone?"

"Normally we'd all be at yoga, but the flood put an end to our classes."

"Not necessarily," said Fen. "I have a hunch. If I'm right, there's a job for you."

"Do you want me to come to your place?"

He pondered the question, but not for long. "Get dressed and meet me at the donut shop downtown. I'll have Lou meet us there after she calls me back."

Fen struggled to get the elastic knee brace on because of his damp skin. He considered calling Chief Strange and having him meet them downtown but decided against it. It was possible, but not likely, that Cindi and Holly's disappearance had a simple explanation. Every fiber of Fen's being told him something evil was afoot, but he needed facts before he called for help.

Fully dressed with file folder in hand he slammed the front door shut behind him. Once in his truck, he looked in the rearview mirror and noticed he'd not combed his wet hair. He made do with his fingers and even managed an almost-straight part. A stoplight near the donut shop brought him to a halt. His phone came alive with a call from Lou.

"The back door's kicked in. Signs of a struggle. There's a zip-tie on the bedroom floor."

Fen released a loud groan. "I should have seen it before this morning." He righted himself emotionally. "Get to the donut shop downtown as quick as you can. Bailey's on her way. I think the killer has both Cindi and Holly."

"Who are you talking about? What's the killer's name?"

"I'll explain later."

His mind was a jumble of facts. Things were moving fast, too fast, but he couldn't control that part. He'd have to react to situations as they arose.

It didn't surprise him that Bailey beat him to the donut shop, but what came as a shock was she'd not come alone. Next to her at a table sat Candice. Like her late mother, she looked beautiful with or without makeup.

Fen approached with eyebrows raised, asking Bailey for an explanation without using words. She understood and said, "Candice had bad dreams last night and Mrs. Dillworth gave her a hard time."

Candice shook her head. "That old woman must eat sauerkraut three meals a day." She looked into Fens eyes. "If you're going to catch the person who killed my mother, I'd like to be there when you put him in handcuffs."

Fen took a seat. "I'm a broken-down former sheriff with a bad knee. I'm not planning on putting handcuffs on anyone."

She stared with piercing eyes and a knowing smile. "Good try, Mr. Maguire. My mother passed down to me whatever allows me to see right through a man. Right now, I see a hunter."

He realized it was a waste of time to try to deceive her. "You're right, I'm hunting this morning, but that doesn't mean I'll be the one who captures the prey. In fact I'll do everything in my power to make sure it's someone else." He paused. "Another job of a really skilled hunter is to make sure the prey doesn't hurt anyone. If you're with Bailey and I give her something to do, I need you to stay far away. You may know how to read some men, but she has skills and instincts that you don't have."

As they were coming to a meeting of the minds, he noticed

Bailey shift her gaze to the door. In walked Officer Brent Craven, flag-pole thin and looking tired in his baggy uniform. Fen motioned him over to the table.

"Let me get coffee and something to eat."

"Bailey will get it for you. Tell her what you want."

Bailey stood and asked Fen what he wanted. "Coffee and a dozen assorted pastries." He took out a wad of bills from the front pocket of his jeans and handed them to her. "This has the makings of a busy day. We'd better get fortified."

Candice also rose from her chair. "I'll go with you Bailey. I love sausage and cheese kolaches."

"Me too," said Brent. He shifted his gaze to Fen. "Since I last saw you, I strained the triceps muscle of my left arm lifting weights. I thought I was going to drop the bar on my head."

Once again, the gears meshed together in Fen's brain. His gaze narrowed. "Did you ever add any items to the list of bars that might have been used to kill Jewell?"

"No, but after I hurt my arm, I think we could add a weight bar to the list."

Chapter Twenty-Seven

F en's plan jelled into something that might work, but he didn't discuss it with the thin, young officer. Bailey and Candice returned to the table with a box of goodies and joined the conversation. He put his elbows on the table and spoke in a low voice to all three. "I think I know where Holly and her mom are, but I need to make sure before calling in the cavalry." He looked at Officer Craven. "Do you know where the new gym in town is?"

"Sure. It's on Sidney Baker Street, the main drag coming from the interstate into downtown. It's close to the Y.O. Resort."

"I need you and Bailey to get there as quick as possible and see if they're open."

Brent no longer looked tired. "What's going on?"

"I believe Cindi and her daughter have been abducted. They may be at the new gym."

Brents eyes widened in alarm. "I just got off patrol. On my last run through town I saw the owner's car pull in."

"Could you tell if anyone was with him?"

Brent's head shook, causing his baseball cap to slide farther down on his head. Even his cap was too big.

"He drove around back and was too far away for me to get a good look." Brent scratched his chin. "Now that I think about it he always parks in front of the building."

Fen shifted his gaze to Bailey. "Get there quick with Brent and take your SUV. I'll follow with Candice. Go around back. Make sure no one inside can see Brent's uniform. I'll go to the front door and cause a distraction while you open the rear door if it's locked."

"Does she have a key?" asked Brent.

"Don't ask," said Bailey.

Fen glanced at the box of treats. "Everyone get something to eat. We need to get our blood sugar up so we can think clearly." Once they cleared the front door, he said to Bailey, "Don't do anything foolish unless you want to answer to Thelma."

"She'll blame you."

Brent asked, "Don't I need to call this in?"

"Not until we know they're in the building. He might have taken them somewhere else."

Once outside, a holler stopped everyone in their tracks. "Don't even think about leaving without me," shouted Lou as she sprinted toward them. "I've had a belly-full of your secrets, Fen Maguire. Tell me what's going on."

"Get in. This story will go above the fold on the front page."

Lou glanced at Candice and then back at him. "Is she coming with us?"

"I certainly am," replied Candice. "I'm calling shotgun. You can get in the back seat."

Lou muttered, "Oh for heaven's sake. I'm back in high school."

Bailey's vehicle took off like a cheetah after an impala with

Fen pushing his truck hard to keep her in sight. He followed distant taillights until Bailey turned on the street a half block south of the gym. He spoke to himself as much as to Lou and Candice. "She's gone past the building. Wait, she's turning. There must be an alley in the back of the building or some other way of getting back there."

He'd already slowed and applied brakes in order to turn into the parking lot. It was important to make their approach not look like a NASCAR pit stop. Easing his truck into a parking spot one row in front of the curb, he took out his phone and saw that Bailey had texted an update.

Car's here. Calling for backup.

Fen made a snap decision and returned Bailey's text.

Call it in as a burglary. Tell officers not to come in hot.

Understood. And you?

Creating diversion.

He opened his door but not before Lou and Candice did the same. "Stop!" he shouted. "This guy is a killer."

Candice led the way with Lou telling her to stop. A slip on the asphalt while getting out of the truck made him wish he'd strapped on his metal knee brace instead of the elastic one. It wasn't searing pain, but enough to make him realize he'd need ice packs tonight. His truck door slammed shut at the same moment Candice banged on the building's door.

He whispered a mantra that came to mind. "Acknowledge, adjust, adapt, and overcome." Walking stiff-legged to the front door, he stepped in front of the two women and ordered Candice back to the truck. She didn't have time to respond before the door swung open and he stared down the barrel of a chrome-plated pistol.

Lou let out a yelp. All he could do was swallow a lump, but Candice ignored the threat and took a step forward. "Hi, Roy. We're here for yoga. I lost your card so we couldn't call you."

"No classes today," said the man as he lowered the pistol, but didn't stand aside.

Fen found his voice. "No classes this early is music to my ears. I don't know if you remember me, but we met last week. I'm the art teacher for the two-week summer class and art competition. Our class is almost over and I thought I'd give your class a try before I left town. We're going to announce winners on Saturday."

He gave Fen a hard stare. "Are you a judge?"

"Not exactly, but I'll be allowed to share my opinion of each student with the three decision-makers."

The hulk of a man rubbed his chin with the hand not holding the pistol. "I need to talk to you."

Lou spoke up. "I'm Lou Cooper, one of the judges."

Fitness instructor and gym owner Roy Shanks raised his eyebrows. "Where are my manners? Come in. We need to talk. I've developed a strong interest in art. After all, Kerrville is quite the gathering place for artists and sculptors."

With the pistol in his meaty hand, the three had no choice but to enter. With his suspicions confirmed that the man before them was Roger Slade, Fen had to think fast. "Uh... Roy. If we're going to discuss the competition, it would be best if Candice waited for us in the truck. As you already know, she's a competitor."

Roger, AKA Roy, stayed silent too long, staring at the

young woman who had a striking resemblance to her deceased mother. Finally he gave his head a slow shake. "No. She looks like the type of girl who already knows she's one of the top competitors. I have some questions for her."

The situation went from bad to worse. The plan for him to create a simple distraction while Officer Craven got the drop on the man he now knew was Roger Slade, ex-con and Holly's father, was in shambles. He had Lou and Candice to worry about now, not to mention Bailey and Officer Craven. Were they in the building already or was Bailey having trouble picking the lock?

Slade turned a key in the metal frame of the glass door. If Fen was right, two hostages now numbered five, with a good possibility that Bailey and Brent were stuck in the back parking lot. Slade lifted his left hand and said, "Go straight and turn left when you get to the recumbent bicycles. The light is better in the area with free weights."

Lou took Candice by the arm, guiding her, while Fen limped along with Slade keeping enough distance between them that any sudden move would be his last. Everything was in Slade's favor. His strength and skills could end lives without firing a shot, which presented a seemingly insurmountable advantage.

"Time," whispered Fen to himself. "I have to buy some time."

Lou turned the corner and led the way into an L-shaped room with chrome-plated bars, padded benches with hooks to hold the bars, and racks of free weights.

Fen knew his job was to keep Slade from ending multiple lives. He kept his bum leg straight and eased down on the bench with a shiny, silver-colored bar on it. "Whew, I should have had this knee properly fixed a long time ago."

Slade tilted his head. "What did you do to it?"

How much did the ex-con know? Was this a test to see if he'd lie? In less time than it took to blink, Fen came up with a mostly accurate answer. "A very mad woman shot me." He issued a laugh that sounded insincere. "It's not as bad as it sounds. She meant to hit her husband. You know, wrong place, wrong time. I'm going to have a knee replacement this coming winter." He moved on after taking a quick breath. "I used to be in pretty good shape. Can't wait to go through rehab and lose some of this flab."

Slade didn't react to the attempt to make conversation and buy time. Instead, he turned to Lou. "Do you judge many contests?"

"When I'm not teaching."

"Where do you teach?"

"The Chicago Institute of Art."

Fen had to hand it to Lou. She was quick with a lie. But he knew lies came with peril.

"Is Whistler's painting of the woman in white still on display there?"

Lou swallowed and Fen opened his mouth to speak, but Candice beat him to it. "Everyone knows *Woman in White* stays at the National Gallery of Art." She looked around and asked, "Did Holly come here this morning?"

Slade's eyes narrowed as he raised the pistol to point the business end at Candice. "You and the fake judge have a seat on the bench next to the former cop." He shifted his gaze to Fen. "Real slow, raise your hands and stand up."

Fen did as he was told.

"Pull your shirt up and turn a slow circle."

Again, he complied and was thankful he hadn't grabbed his pistol on the way out of the condo.

"That's good. Sit down again and keep your hands on your knees." Slade walked to an enormous poster of himself with muscles rippling as he did a biceps curl with an obscene amount of weight.

Fen hadn't noticed the door frame and the knob that the poster camouflaged. He nodded to the poster. "Was that taken right after you got out of prison?"

The ex-con answered with a churlish smile. He turned the handle and light spilled into the room. "Come on out, darling."

A voice spoke from inside the room. "I'm not your darling."

"I wasn't talking to you, Cindi. You and Holly get out here before someone gets hurt."

Dressed in sleepwear, mother and daughter came into the room and closed the door behind them.

"On the bench, next to the others," said Slade.

Out of the corner of his eye, Fen could see Cindi and Holly sit on a bench with a rack holding a bar with several hundred pounds of weights in hooks. At that moment he knew exactly how Jewell died. He asked, "Was that the same bench and bar you used to kill Jewell?"

Evil shone in Slade's eyes. "It was the bench you're sitting on. So easy to kill her. She wanted a fling and was into new experiences. The idea of coming here late at night was all hers."

While Candice pummeled him with words, Fen shifted his gaze back to the poster. He spoke over Candice's rant. "Were you able to get steroids in prison, or did you have to wait until you were out?"

A chuckle preceded the answer. "What do you think?"

The room quieted as Candice's rough words were replaced with soft sobs. He thought back to the report from Candy. "You and your buddies were trying to stay alive. They had connections and all it cost you was a few years of helping them make money after they released you. That tells me you scored steroids in prison and kept building your body after your release."

"You're smarter than you look, but not smart enough to save yourself and everyone but Holly."

It was at that moment it became clear that Roy Shanks, originally known as Roger Slade, had fried his brain on steroids. What could he do besides delay the process and pray for help to arrive?

Chapter Twenty-Eight

The need to prolong the exchange outweighed the desire to spare Candice's grief. With a tilt of his head, Fen said, "It's obvious you know who I am and that I like to study homicides. Exactly how did you kill Jewell and why?" His gaze rested on the weights and silver bar. "Did you spot her with more weight than any woman her size could budge and let it crush her?"

A sinister smile telegraphed Slade's pleasure as he explained. "I told her it would be something special if she watched me work out first. I loaded the bar with plenty of weight on each side and did enough to show her what a real man looks like. Then I said it was her turn and took off all the weights. At first she didn't want to, but I told her I'd stand over her instead of behind her. I slipped off my shirt and flexed my arms and pecks. That's all it took to get her on the bench. We raised and lowered the bar a few times together before I put it on her throat and pressed down. It didn't take long."

"I can see it," said Fen in a voice he hoped would drown out Candice's sobs. "I have to admit that's a novel way of doing away with someone, but I'm still not clear about why you wanted her dead."

Slade pointed to Holly. "I did it for my daughter."

"I don't even know you," said Holly, her voice cracking.

"You don't yet, but that's all going to change."

"Over my dead body," said Cindi.

Slade's response came like a crack of a whip. "You just predicted your future. I'll be glad to snap your neck like a twig. In fact, I'll take care of you first." He shook his head in mock disappointment. "I came here to see if you still loved me. I guess that boat sailed a long time ago with plenty of help from your father poisoning your mind. He was supposed to be the first on my list to take care of but that Rose Cunningham woman came on to me in a bar and I thought she was the Key woman. I recognized her from Facebook photos."

"I was right," said Fen with too much glee in his voice to fit the occasion. "Rose was a simple case of mistaken identity."

"Collateral damage," said Slade without a hint of remorse in his voice.

He had to keep Slade talking about the case and give him opportunities to show how superior he believed himself to be. "How did you get a new identity?"

Slade cut his eyes to look at Fen. "You ask a lot of questions."

Lou jumped in. "He's lousy at it too. I'm an award-winning reporter and I know the type of man people like to read about. Believe me, they'll be talking about you for years. You'll be a hero in people's eyes. Yours will be a story of how a vicious, greedy man cheated you out of the love of a beautiful young woman. He also kept you from your child and even forced you to leave the state."

Fen caught on to the game of delay Lou was playing. "Did

you know Stony had private detectives keeping tabs on you for years after you moved to California?"

"That's not all he did. He fixed it where I couldn't get a decent job or hold one for more than a few months."

Fen wasn't sure if that was true but it didn't matter. If Slade was talking he wasn't killing. Fen asked, "Is it true Stony stopped keeping tabs on you after five years?"

"The only reason he did was because I went to prison. Another set-up to make me suffer."

"Lies and more lies," said Cindi. "I'd finished my degree and was halfway through my MBA by then. I lost all interest in you before I finished high school. Daddy may have been strict on me, but I can see now that he loved me enough to protect me from an animal like you." She took a breath. "Look at you. All pumped up with muscles thinking you're God's gift to women. You may have convinced yourself that I loved you, but I was too young and dumb to know what love really is."

Fen straightened his leg which caught Slade's attention and focused his ire on someone besides Cindi. The words flew from Fen's mouth in order to occupy the giant's mind with something besides murder. "Did you leave the note in Cindi's door?"

The question may not have stopped Slade in his tracks but it slowed him down. Lou added, "That's a detail I need to include in the book I'm going to write about you. Tell me about the note."

"It doesn't matter now, but yes. I left a note. That was before I realized how much Cindi reminds me of her father." His icy gaze passed from one person to the next, while his thumb rubbed the hammer on the pistol.

"Wait," said Fen in a voice that rose to a shout. "I still don't know why you killed Jewell. I'm asking as a student of criminology. Explain why she had to die."

"You seem to have all the answers. You tell me."

Fen pursed his lips and gave a nod. "Correct me if I'm wrong... Jewell had two priorities in her life: herself and her daughter, Candice."

A slow nod came from Slade so Fen continued, "There's no need to go over her exploits with men but she didn't fool you. You refused to be another notch on her bedpost. She wanted a boy-toy but you wanted something else. That rules out sex or money. A guy like you had women falling at your feet. You didn't need her money because you left California with loads of cash." He paused, took in a deep breath, and said, "The only thing left is the way she treated your daughter. It was one thing for Stony to treat you like scum, but when you found out how Jewell was rigging contests for Candice, you had to put a stop to her."

Another nod.

Fen followed with a question. "How long have you kept up with Holly?"

He shrugged. "I took classes in prison and learned how to surf the 'net. It's amazing how easy it was to follow Cindi. She loves to post things on Facebook. I never contacted Holly or Cindi until this week. As for Jewell, that was easy. Cindi told me all about her online. I made up the name Roy Shanks and became a friend of hers."

"Ah, I should have known." Fen tapped his fingers on his thighs. "Help me on this one. How long did it take you to figure out Holly and Candice weren't friendly competitors in their private school, especially in art contests?"

"Candice was always the winner, never my Holly. I blew it off for a year or two, but then I figured her mom had to be fixing it for her to win every time."

"And it gnawed on you and brought back memories of how Stony treated you."

His words exploded from his mouth. "Wouldn't it make

you furious if someone messed over your kid? I studied art enough to know what's good and what's trash. Holly should've had her share of blue ribbons, but the only time that happened was on the rare occasion when Holly entered a contest that Candice didn't."

"So you moved to Texas to settle the score?"

"It's what fathers do for their kids. I killed Jewel so Holly could compete on a level field."

"You're crazy," said Cindi. "I knew what Jewell was doing and talked to Holly about it."

"It didn't bother me," said Holly. "I love to paint, and so does Candice. Who cares about ribbons and trophies?"

"I do," shouted Slade. "Don't you understand? I killed for you. Now... I'm tired of all this talk. No one is going to talk me out of what I'm going to do."

Fen realized that Cindi's inarticulate mental diagnosis of Slade being crazy was spot on. Years of taking performance-enhancing drugs had altered his body and his mind. Perhaps they still had a chance if he could delay a little longer. Before realizing what he was saying, he blurted out, "Me first."

Slade pointed his pistol at him. "I'd rather take care of the one who kept my daughter from me first."

Fen spoke quickly. "Even though I have a bad knee, I'm still your biggest threat." He nodded to the women on the benches. "They could all rush you at the same time and you'd swat them away like flies."

An evil laugh came from the deranged hulk of a man. He waved his pistol in Fen's direction. "Get up."

Fen held up his hands. "Hold on a minute. If I'm going to be first, the least you can do is make it interesting, like you did for Jewell."

A wicked grin parted his lips. "What did you have in

mind?" He paused. "You can forget about me standing over you with my shirt off and helping you with the bar."

After rubbing his chin, Fen said, "Let's do something original that doesn't make noise or a big mess." He snapped his fingers. "I know. I haven't lifted weights in forever. If I'm going to meet my maker, I'd like to know how much I can lift on a simple biceps curl. I'll start off with ten pounds on each side to warm up and add weight until I max out."

"Then what?" asked Slade.

"Then it's your turn to get creative. All I ask is that you make it quick and quiet."

Slade pointed. "There's the bar. Carry it to the rubber mats and put ten pounds on each end. Make sure you tighten them down good." He looked at the other four. "Go to the far corner and sit down. Everyone but Holly will take their turn after I'm finished with him. Honey, you'll go with me today."

The pistol in his hand made compliance a simple choice. Fen toted the bar to an area in the middle of the room. He chose a spot near a rack of weights. They varied in size from small and thin, to ones that made his back hurt looking at them. He selected two ten-pound weights, slid them over each end of the bar, and tightened the wing nut on the clamp that held them in place. It wasn't much weight, which was good, considering his knee throbbed when he picked it up.

Slade stood between him and the door covered with the poster of the likeness of the man who intended to continue his killing spree. After three reps, Fen noticed the doorknob turn. He spoke in a loud voice. "I'm feeling pretty good, but it will help if I have moral support when I add weight. Weren't any of you cheerleaders?"

"I was," said Lou.

"I'm going to put another fifty pounds on each side. I'm not sure my knee will hold out, so this will be my last lift. When I lift, give me a good, loud shout of encouragement. I'd hate to go out of this world thinking I'm a failure."

Slade slipped the pistol into the waistband of his spandex shorts and folded thick arms over his massive chest. Fen slid two twenty-five-pound weights on each end of the bar. He tightened the left side and pretended to tighten the right. Reaching down, he grabbed and shouted. "Is everyone ready?"

"Ready," shouted Lou.

"On three. One... two... THREE!"

Lou and Holly let out a scream as he brought the bar to his waist. His knee buckled, and he joined his scream with the others. He stumbled forward and turned ninety degrees to his left. His right hand dipped as he jerked up with his left. To his surprise, he'd judged the distance between him and Slade correctly. The weights on the right side of the bar slid off and came crashing down on Slade's right foot like they had a built-in guidance system.

Lying on the mat, Fen looked through cloudy eyes to see the door with the poster fly open. Officer Brent Craven came in with pistol drawn. Slade hopped on one foot, turning to face the threat. His hand was already on the pistol.

Brent hollered, "Don't do it!"

Two shots rang out in close succession. Slade spun in a circle and dropped to the ground as his pistol slid across the room. Blood flowed from his right shoulder.

Candice and Holly ignored the danger and came toward the fallen man. They each picked up a twenty-five-pound weight and moved to where Slade reeled in pain. They looked at each other, nodded, and bombed his knees with the weights, making sure they landed with the edge down.

Fen wondered if Slade's knees, toes, and shoulder hurt as much as his own knee did. He dismissed the thought and motioned for Lou to come to him.

She knelt beside him, as did Bailey. A tsunami of pain swept over him. "I told you this story would go above the fold."

"How's the knee?" asked Bailey.

"It's gone." He reached out and took her hand as another wave brought white dots before his eyes.

"We'll get you to the hospital," said Lou.

He shook off the desire to slip into the black hole of unconsciousness. "When you write this, make it about hometown heroes. Give Officer Craven and Chief Strange the credit."

"I understand."

Bailey squeezed his hand. "Don't worry about the rest of the summer shows. I'll do them by myself."

He pointed to Holly and Candice. "Those two need to work on their caricatures. Teach them what I taught you, and have fun."

The next face to look down at him belonged to Chief Strange. "Ambulance is on the way."

Fen nodded. "Looks like I'll be leaving town before I planned. My orthopedic surgeon told me he'd move me to the front of the line whenever I'm ready."

"I'll stop by the hospital and get a statement from you." He took a breath. "Thanks for saving my job."

"I was lucky."

Ben Strange swung his head from side to side. "You made your own luck."

Chapter Twenty-Nine

The door to the hospital room opened and a familiar face peeked in. "Are you decent?"

"I'm decent until they make me sit on the side of the bed. Someone left the back door open on this gown." Fen looked at Bailey's smiling face. "Please tell me you came to help me escape from this high-priced jail."

She moved to his bedside. "The nurse told me one sign of a patient getting well is how much they complain." She looked down at the lump under his sheet. It was several inches thicker than the other leg. "Your surgeon said it was a miracle you stood the pain as long as you did. Everything was an absolute mess. Now there's titanium and plastic."

He hadn't noticed it until now, but Bailey held a white paper sack. "Did Thelma send me goodies?"

"It depends on how you define *goodies*. She's worried about the anesthesia and pain medicine making you constipated. High-fiber cookies are in the bag I left in my SUV. I tried one. It tasted like molasses and sawdust." She shook the sack. "I stopped by a bakery. There're three chocolate-chunk cookies for you that are big as a salad plate."

"How many were in the bag when you left the shop?"

She grinned. "Five. One for the trip here, and another for the trip home. You get the rest."

He worried with the identification band on his wrist. "Tell me about the contest in Kerrville. Who won?"

She moved to a recliner on the other side of the bed, speaking as she went. "Candice took third place while Holly placed second. They were both great paintings, but the one that P.B. submitted was so detailed and original, it won hands down."

"I'm glad the judges looked past her clothes and makeup."

"They didn't have to. She wore white slacks, a pastel print blouse, and none of the goth makeup. I talked to her after the competition and she said the Adams Family look helped her get into the theme of her painting. It allowed her to see the dark side of life."

Fen raised his eyebrows. "Deep for a high school girl."

"She was having a hard time identifying with hardships, death, and disappointments. She also wanted to emphasize that things aren't as they seem."

"She never would let me see the painting. What did it look like?"

"She used the dam to divide the painting into two scenes. Below it was a swift, dangerous river, but in the shallows children and two dogs splashed and played."

"Sounds nice."

Bailey added, "There was a couple having a picnic. They were flanked on two sides by cactus, but they were on a bed of green grass and their body language spoke of relaxed contentment."

"What did you see on the lake side of the dam?"

"Contradictions all over the place. It was a gorgeous setting, but there was a dead fish on the bank, a child crying over a broken toy, a buzzard flying overhead, and trash overflowing from a rusty barrel. If you looked closely, you could make out a man walking away from a crying woman."

He summarized. "P.B. made herself into a dualistic contradiction so she could create a painting that told the same story. Very smart." He pushed a button and raised his upper body. "What did you learn from her painting?"

Bailey didn't hesitate. "Tell at least one story in everything I do, even caricatures."

"You'll go far if you do that." He used his elbows to lift himself higher in the bed. "Speaking of caricatures, are Holly and Candice going to do shows with you this summer?"

Bailey leaned back in the recliner. "Candice rented an awesome apartment in San Marcos for the rest of the summer. We'll use it as a home base for weekend shows up and down I-35. They've also decided to be roommates at the University of Texas this fall."

"What about you?"

"I have other plans, but for the rest of the summer, it's every weekend with those two. It'll be fun for a couple of months, but by the time their semester starts, they'll be ready to move on and I'll need to paint full time."

"Still no desire to go to college?"

"I'll take a couple of online classes, but I'm still not sold on getting a degree. The fall and Christmas shows will be here before you know it and there's so many places in this big ol' state we haven't been." She cast a smile his way. "Besides, the surgeon says your rehab will take longer than usual because you did so much additional damage to your knee. Do you really want Thelma taking you to physical therapy?"

A shiver ran down his spine.

"Anything else I missed this past week while I've been drugged?"

She dry-washed her hands, which was her way of telling him she had bad news.

The door swung open and Lou strolled in. "Is he still talking crazy and slurring his words?"

"No, he's not," said Fen with sarcasm seasoning his words. "Come in and tell me why Bailey's wringing her hands."

Lou flicked the comment away. "It's nothing to a rich man like you."

He groaned and waited to hear the damage to his bank account.

"You may not remember everything that happened at Slade's gym." She tilted her head. "Do you recall hearing two shots when you were on the gym floor?"

He thought back. "There was a lot of hollering and we belted out a scream. That's about it." He narrowed his gaze.

Lou asked, "Do you remember what kind of pistol Slade carried?"

"Big and chrome plated. It was at least a .357 magnum."

"Close," said Lou. "It was a .44 Magnum."

Fen swallowed. "Big guns make enormous holes. What did it hit?"

Lou used her hand to add a gesture to her words. "It shattered a plate-glass window at the front of the store before it hit your truck. Went through the radiator, cooling fan, and cracked the engine block. It takes one heck of a weapon to do that much damage."

His head sank into his pillow as he whispered, "Slade killed my truck."

Lou seemed to enjoy telling the story. "Yep. Killed it dead. There was oil and coolant all over the parking lot. Looked like it bled to death. The insurance adjuster declared it DOA."

Bailey added, "Don't worry, you won't be able to drive for a while. This will give you plenty of time to decide what you want next."

A knock on the metal frame of the door took his mind off the loss of his truck. In walked Chief Strange, wearing jeans, boots, and a short-sleeve shirt. "If I'm intruding, I can grab a cup of coffee."

Fen waved him in. "Come join the wake. I'm grieving the loss of my truck."

"You're just now learning about that?"

Lou explained. "It took several days to get the swelling down enough so they could operate. He tried to back out of the operation, so his doctor ordered something that took the fight out of him."

Bailey jumped in. "His knee was such a mess the surgery took almost twice as long as usual."

"Enough about me, my knee, and my dearly departed truck," said Fen. "How are things in Kerrville?"

Lou moved to the other side of the bed, making room for Chief Strange to draw near.

He responded with, "Things are peaceful and good. The mayor's office hasn't summoned me since they transferred you here."

"When was that?"

"Last Saturday. They gave you happy juice in your IV and brought you in by helicopter."

His mouth hinged open as Lou chuckled and explained. "Chuck and Candy thought you needed a first-class ride to Austin. I told them they should save the money and let Bailey bring you in the back of her SUV."

He considered her attempt at humor but had to agree that the first-class transport was a waste. "I wish I could have vetoed that decision. They could have replaced my truck with a new one for what they spent on a medical helicopter."

He took in a full breath and let it out. "Oh, well. Hard come, easy go." He refocused on Chief Strange. "What happened after I passed out?"

"Slade went to the hospital to get patched up. His right arm is in a sling and both legs are in casts from toes to thigh. We transferred him to county jail yesterday and his muscles are shrinking as we speak. He's being held without bond and the mayor and DA are trying to get him to trial as soon as possible. They want to get him to prison so the state will be stuck with his medical care." He pointed at Fen's elevated leg. "The doctors think Slade will need two artificial knees."

What felt like ice water spilling down his back shook Fen as he considered two knee replacements.

Lou said, "It couldn't happen to a nicer guy."

In a sudden change of direction, Ben glanced at Bailey. "Does he know what you did for Ray-Ray?"

Fen shook his head. "Is he out of jail?" He looked at Bailey. "What did you do?"

"Nothing special. I bought him a huge umbrella that attaches to a stool. They released him Friday afternoon and he was singing and playing his guitar by that night. The weather called for it to be hot and sunny all weekend and I didn't want him to roast. Candice tried to give him money but he wouldn't take it. By the time he finished playing that night he'd earned enough for a hotel room, a good meal, and enough for breakfast on Saturday."

Ben added, "The time in jail scared him down to the soles of his sandals. He played all weekend and his A.A. sponsor came from San Antonio and picked him up Sunday afternoon before the booths shut down."

A few seconds passed in silence before Fen asked, "What else did I miss?"

Ben held up his index finger. "You haven't missed it yet, but Officer Craven will soon be Sergeant Craven."

Nods of approval came from all.

Two women dressed in scrubs came through the door. The one built like a linebacker took charge. "Mr. Maguire, we're from physical therapy. It's time for you to take your first steps on that new knee."

Bailey rose from the recliner like she sat on a tack. Lou waved and headed for the door. She looked at Chief Strange. "If you don't want to hear a man scream like a little girl, you'd better come with us and get a cup of coffee."

Ben stuck out his hand for him to shake. "Thanks again." He turned to leave then spun back to face him. "By the way, my aunt Lois told me to tell you she wishes you a speedy recovery."

Fen searched his mind and came up blank. "Your aunt Lois?"

"Lois Dillworth. She said you're a man she'll never forget."

Fraud, deception, murder... what else awaits Fen along the banks of the muddy Wichita?

Private detective Fen Maguire is asked to investigate a cold case involving a missing real estate broker who swindled millions from local residents. When the reporter who wrote exposé articles on the fraud victims is found dead, the waters surrounding Fen's case get even murkier.

With the police refusing to believe there's a connection, Fen is left on his own to follow the trail to the money... and the killer.

Scan the image below to get your copy or go to brucehammack.com/books/murder-on-the-wichita/.

Thank you for reading *Murder On The Guadalupe*. I hope Fen and his team kept you turning the pages to find out whodunit! If you loved it, please consider leaving a review at your favorite retailer, Bookbub or Goodreads. Your reviews help other readers discover their next great mystery!

If you would like to get in on the fun that surrounds the writing of my books, join my mailing list. You'll be among the first to know about new releases, discounts and recommendations. After you sign up you'll receive the first perk of being a Mystery Insider, the prequel to the Fen Maguire Mysteries!

Happy Reading!

Bruce

You may scan below to sign up or go to brucehammack.com/the-fen-maguire-mysteries-prequel.

About The Author

Drawing from his extensive background in criminal justice, Bruce Hammack writes contemporary, clean read detective and crime mysteries. A huge fan of Hercule Poirot and Sherlock Holmes, he believes the world can never have enough whodunits!

He is the author of the Smiley and McBlythe Mysteries, the Fen Maguire Mysteries, the Star of Justice series and the Detective Steve Smiley Mysteries. Having lived in eighteen cities around the world, he now shares his home in the Texas hill country with his wife of thirty-plus years and an aging gray cat with one fang and a sketchy attitude.

Follow Bruce on Amazon, Bookbub and Goodreads for the latest new release info and recommendations. Learn more at brucehammack.com.